ACHE

MARLEY VALENTINE

usa today bestselling author
MARLEY VALENTINE

Copyright © 2021 by Marley Valentine

No part of this publication may be reproduced, distributed, or transmitted in any form or by any means, including photocopying, recording, or other electronic or mechanical methods, without the prior written permission of the publisher, except in the case of brief quotations embodied in critical reviews and certain other noncommercial uses permitted by copyright law.
This novel is a work of fiction. While reference may be made to actual historical events or existing locations, the names, characters, places and incidents are products of the author's imagination. Any resemblance to people either living or deceased, business establishments, events or locales is purely coincidental and not intended by the author.
Any trademarks, service marks, product names or named features are assumed to be the property of their respective owners, and are only used for reference. There is no implied endorsement if any of these terms are used.

Cover design by PopKitty Designs
Cover Models & Photographer: Chip and Alexx Pons
Edited by Shauna Stevenson at Ink Machine Editing
& ellie mclove at My Brother's Editor
Proofreading by Hawkeyes Proofing & Jodi Prellwitz Duggan

This book contains mature content.

DEDICATION

Steph. This one is for you.

I feel you everywhere, I look for you in everything.

BUTTERFLIES RISING

DEAR READER

Gael and Jordan's story was originally published as a twenty-five thousand word novella called Regrets & Resolutions.

Please be informed the original novella has been turned into a full length novel, with over fifty thousand words of brand new content.

Some of the original story was expanded, changed , added and/or removed for the greater good of the story. There is also a trigger warning for the mention of an off the page miscarriage.

With that said, I hope you enjoy Ache, an emotional, friends-to lovers, gay romance.

1

———

JORDAN

BUZZ. Buzz. Buzz.

The incessant sound of something vibrating beside me stirs me from my sleep.

Buzz. Buzz. Buzz.

Extending my arm, I feel around for the offending sound but come up empty.

Where the fuck's my nightstand?

Sluggishly, I prop up my head and look around my room, only to realize this isn't my room. Or my bed. Turning, my eyes land on the body of a man I remember thoroughly enjoying last night.

More than once.

Fuck. Frankie.

Frankie, my friend—and I use that term loosely—with benefits' eyes flicker open. A slow, tired smile spreads over his face as last night's bad decision begins to throb at my temples.

"Morning," he says lazily, moving himself closer to me.

Not quite down for a repeat, I lean in the opposite direction, just out of his reach.

"Where are you going?" He sighs, not surprised or deterred by my attempt at rejection. "I thought we could go another round. Or two."

Sitting up, I throw my legs over the edge of the bed and give him my back. "It's Christmas Day, Frankie. I've got places to be and people to see."

"Ah, yes. Christmas with your surrogate family." He laughs humorlessly. "Run along to Gael."

Stiffening at his tone, I turn to look behind me and glare at him. "Why are you such a prick?"

"Because you make it so easy," he answers, throwing back the covers. "Playing second best grates on a man, you know?"

Ignoring him, I rise off the bed and walk around the room naked, trying to find all my belongings from the night before.

"I'm going to have a shower," he announces, standing in the bathroom doorway. "Do me a favor, yeah?"

Picking my jeans up off the floor, I keep my eyes on him expectantly.

"Don't call me tonight when you're all alone in your bed."

He slams the door, leaving me alone and angry that he knows me so well and guilty for not being the only asshole under this roof.

Sliding into my jeans, I drag them up my legs and fasten the button. I thread my arms into my t-shirt and head for the bathroom.

The air is thick with steam, the glass door covered in fog, but not enough to miss Frankie standing there with his head down under the spray and soapy hands roaming around his lithe, toned body.

In another life, I would step into the shower and spend

the whole day getting lost in the man of my choice. Lost in the man who was willing to take all of me and to give me every part of him in return.

But we don't have that.

By choice and out of habit, I don't have that with anybody, and the only person who I would want it with isn't an option.

Instead, Frankie is the guy on the side who I treat like shit, showing him the very worst parts of myself.

The parts that are cold and angry. The parts that have been hardened by life. The parts that don't love and don't let anybody else in.

I hate every single one of those things, but I can't change them. I've tried, but I can't. Not for Frankie. Not for anyone.

Except him.

I shake the errant thought from my mind and knock on the door to announce my arrival. "Frankie."

He stills, but he doesn't look at me.

"I'm sorry," I say. He angles his head my way, his features a lot softer than they were only moments ago. "Have a Merry Christmas."

Without waiting for an answer, I offer a sad smile and move to close the door.

"Jordan, wait," he calls out. "I'm sorry too. You know I can be a catty bitch."

The side of my mouth tips upward in a smirk. "Well, that's an understatement, but I get it. We don't need to keep doing this." I swallow hard. "*I* don't need to keep doing this to *you*."

"It takes two to tango," he supplies with a shrug. "But, yeah, maybe we should both cool off for a while."

Nodding, I watch as he turns back around, leaving me to get one last look at his wet, sculpted body.

He's gorgeous. Not for the first time, I wish he—even with his catty attitude—was enough.

Sighing, I step out of the bathroom and follow the familiar path down the stairs and straight into the foyer. Grabbing my winter coat off the rack, I button myself up, shove my feet in my boots, and throw my hood over my head before letting myself out.

Seattle winters are brutal, the rain and frigid air hitting me immediately. I turn the car on with my key fob, grateful for life's luxuries, and jog over to it. Sliding in, the heat isn't yet in full force, but the chill in the air is already on its way to defrosting.

Connecting my cell to the car, I notice a message from Gael sitting there unread. Because he's predictable, I don't bother reading it, choosing to call him instead. It's early, but not too early for him.

"Hello." It only takes one ring for his voice to fill my car.

"Hey. What's up?"

"Just checking to see what time you're getting here," he says. "It's still weird not having you sleeping over the night before. The food was amazing."

Gael's family—my surrogate family, as Frankie so eloquently called them— is close. Close enough that we always spend Christmas Eve and Christmas Day at Gael's parents' house, but this year I chose not to partake in the sleepover.

It had been a long time coming. And when my best friend got engaged, I decided, against Gael's unspoken wishes for everything to remain the same, I needed to put some distance between us.

We are grown men with separate lives, who don't

need to get caught up in age-old traditions. Well, at least that's what I tell myself, instead of admitting to how lonely being around Gael and his fiancée really makes me feel.

"We all know the leftovers are where it's at, and it's still early," I inform him. "And I'm not home yet. I have to shower and get all the presents sorted and then I'll be there."

"It is early," he confirms, his voice changing. "And you're not home? Where are you?"

"I slept out," I say, trying to evade the inquisition I know is coming.

"At Frankie's?" he accuses. "I thought you were giving him up."

Gael's disdain for Frankie isn't new. Ever since I hired him as a new agent at my real estate company, Frankie made his interest in me known, and this made Gael's hackles rise. It's not something I understand, nor do I have the need to decipher it. There are some things that best friends don't agree upon, and Frankie is one of them.

"How's Elena?" I ask him, knowing my questioning will distract him enough. "Did she sleep there with you? Did you guys have any luck with her family?"

He lets out a defeated sigh. "She's here. We went to see them last night before coming here, but it didn't really work out."

"Shit. I'm sorry. I know you wanted to make it right with them before the wedding."

"I just feel bad for her," he says solemnly. "I want every-thing to be perfect for her."

In both pain and pride, my chest squeezes at hearing Gael talk about his fiancée. We've been best friends for longer than we haven't. He's always been the only constant in my life, and watching him be happy and fall in love has been a privilege.

Wishing it was me he was happy and in love with has been excruciating.

"I'm sorry," I offer. "If there's anything I can do, just tell me."

Despite my years of pining over Gael, I mean that wholeheartedly. I would go to hell and back for him. No questions asked.

"I just don't want her unnecessarily upset," he adds. "On Christmas or our wedding day."

While the average person doesn't want anybody they love or care about in pain or upset, the way Gael loves is unparalleled.

It didn't matter if it was his family, or Elena, or me. No matter what type of love it was, he did it with his whole heart.

Gael gravitated to anyone or anything that needed his help. He was a protector by nature. An advocate, a friend, a bodyguard. Whenever someone needed something, it was Gael who came to the rescue.

And he had rescued me time and time again.

We were six years old when he told a kid off for trying to steal my lunch. And then fourteen when he backed me in a fight against the power forward of a rival basketball team. We were seventeen when my world turned upside down and he helped me pack my whole life into a suitcase and moved me in with his own family after my parents kicked me out for being gay.

And, unsurprisingly, it was the exact same thing with Elena. Friends first, he was her shoulder to lean on when times were tough. And because he's so good at it, it was inevitable she fell in love with him.

It was a trait of his I now loved and hated equally. In fact, I loved and hated everything about him equally, because it was a rookie mistake, falling in love with your best friend.

It ate at me, but I didn't know how to make it stop. And even now, as he talks my ear off about his fiancée, I still don't know how to not be so irrevocably in love with him.

After all these years, and all the men I'd fooled around with—and there have been plenty—I couldn't shake him. And I try. I was still fucking trying. Trying to move on, trying and failing to find some real connection with Frankie. But my stupid heart won't open up to anyone else, because I can't close the proverbial door on a dream that's never going to come true.

It doesn't help that not a day goes by where we don't talk or see each other. He's in every aspect of my life, and no matter how much it hurts that he isn't in it the way I want him to be, giving him up and walking away from him and the unconventional, almost co-dependent friendship we have isn't an option.

"So, how long do you think it'll be till you get here?" he asks me, moving on from talking about Elena.

"Give me a couple of hours," I concede, hating that I love how needy he can be for me. "I'll try to be quick."

"Okay. Good. I'll see you soon."

Hanging up, I finally pull away from the curb, leaving Frankie and our night together behind.

When I arrive home, I strip down to nothing and have a steaming hot shower. I give my apartment a once over, tidying up the small mess I made while getting ready to go out last night, before organizing and wrapping everybody's Christmas presents.

As grateful as I am for all the things Gael and his family

gave me after I was kicked out of home, there's something about having my own place and reaching a certain level of independence that fills me with a great sense of satisfaction and pride.

Hopeless and scared at seventeen, my life could have very much turned out differently than the one that I have now. But I was stubborn, and I had a best friend and his family who loved me more than my own parents ever would.

And because of them and for them, I have always been determined to make something of myself. I used the opportunity that Gael's parents gave me to live in their home rent free, and I made sure I turned out to be successful enough that I could and would one day repay each and every one of them tenfold.

It was why I loved gift giving. Christmas and birthdays. Mother's Day and Father's Day. If there was ever an excuse to give any one of them a gift, I was on it.

Ever since I got my real estate license, I worked my ass off to get to where I am today and have enough money that I don't want for anything.

I run my own agency, I make my own hours, I have my own house. I have all the things I've ever wanted for myself but nobody to share them with.

So, I give gifts. Elaborate, expensive, unnecessary gifts. Gifts for all the occasions and gifts for no occasions. It was the only love language I knew and one I was able to perfect over the years.

Because all the money and security in the world mean nothing if you don't have anyone to share them with.

And even if it's not the way I want to share my life with Gael, it's undoubtedly better than nothing.

2

———

GAEL

"JORDAN," I hear my father call out. "You're just in time to dress up as Santa."

"Sorry, Papa Bear," he responds. "I don't think these abs of mine can be mistaken for the fat man's beer gut."

Stepping into the foyer, my gaze drifts to the sound of the voices just in time to see Jordan lifting his shirt and showing off his rock-hard body. My eyes do a subtle perusal, taking in his bare skin and all the dips and grooves of his stomach. It's a quick, mastered glance. One that I've practiced and perfected in hopes of hiding the truth for the last ten years. A disinterested look that is the complete opposite of what I really want to do, which is to stare and salivate over how good he always looks.

Dressed in all black and standing tall, it's never a hardship looking at his six-foot-two frame. He works out regularly, we both do, but between his broad shoulders and the ever-present muscle definition that graces every inch of him, it's impossible not to notice every time he steps into the room.

But the showstopper will always be his face. A beautiful

blend of pretty and masculine, he's got the jawline of a Greek god, pillowy pink lips, and gray-blue eyes that change shades with his every mood.

As he runs his hands through his light brown hair and jokes and laughs with my dad, it's an absolute miracle I've managed to hide my attraction to him for all these years.

Instead, I slap on a smile and perfectly time my interruption, laughing at his ridiculousness, because if there's ever a chance to show off what's underneath his clothes, Jordan is the first one to volunteer.

"How many times do I have to tell you, nobody wants to see your body," I say, announcing my presence.

Jordan's eyes dart to mine, an unmistakable flash of heat passing through as he peruses the length of my body, before teasingly biting his bottom lip. "Frankie didn't seem to mind."

I have to bite my tongue and force myself to roll my eyes in jest like I always do when Jordan talks about Frankie. To pretend that the name alone doesn't make my stomach churn and blood boil.

Jordan usually has a revolving door of conquests. He doesn't hide it from me, nor should he, but something about Frankie feels permanent. Much more permanent than anyone before him, and even though I have no right to feel the way I do, I loathe it.

"Oh, Jordan. You're here." A slender arm wraps itself around mine, and I tilt my head to the side to catch my fiancée, Elena, smiling warmly at my best friend. "Are you ready for presents?" she asks him.

He smiles at her, giving her a quick nod, and I narrow my eyes in suspicion, because it's unusual for me to not be the middleman between these two. "What do you two have planned?"

Elena squeezes my arm and places her mouth next to my ear. "I promise it'll be worth it."

Excitedly, she guides me to the family room, the space cluttered with bodies and gifts. My two sisters, Laura and Mariana, and their husbands sitting on the couches, and my nieces and nephews sneakily trying to search through the presents to see which one of them got the most.

It's the same scene every year, our family growing and my childhood home bursting at the seams with both old and new memories. And that includes Jordan. He's been my best friend since kindergarten, and the connection was instant. For all of us.

My parents always treated him like their own, and when his parents found out he was gay in our senior year and kicked him out, there were no questions asked as my mom and dad helped me swoop in to pick up the pieces.

I turn, expecting to find Jordan hot on our heels, but he's still standing in the foyer, his eyes locked on me, his gaze somewhat wistful.

It's a look I see and try to ignore often, because I never know what to make of it.

I tip my head to where everyone's seated. "You coming?"

"Yeah," he says a little too quickly. "I just remembered I forgot something in the car."

"Okay. Do you need help?"

"No," he answers, waving me off. "Just get the kids to start, I'll be back in a minute."

Wanting to wait for him but knowing I should get back to Elena, I let the rising shrieks from the living room pull me in the opposite direction.

"Hey," I shout, when I reach the rest of the family. As a high school teacher, I find myself always responsible for calming down the rowdy children. "You all know the rules. Abuelo and Abuela will only hand out the presents when you're all sitting quietly."

"Uncle Gael," my niece, Sara, whines. At seven, she's the oldest and the self-appointed spokesperson for my other niece and two nephews. "What are we waiting for? We've been waiting all morning."

"We're just waiting for your Uncle Jordan to get something from the car," I explain. It's effortless giving him that title. He's been there for all their births and hasn't missed celebrating a single milestone. Everybody knows he's just as much a part of all our traditions as anybody else under this roof right now. "I'm sure his present will be worth it," I appease.

Huffing, Sara looks behind me, with her hand on her hip, waiting expectantly. When he finally steps into the living room, she doesn't waste time telling him exactly how she feels. "Uncle Jordan, you can't just come late and then go back outside when it's present time."

He passes me by, brushing my shoulder before getting down on a bent knee in front of an irritated Sara. He drags an envelope out of his back pocket and hands it to her. "Maybe this will make it all better?"

Taking my seat next to Elena, I watch Sara's features soften as she plucks the envelope out of his grip. She turns to look back at her mom. "Can I open it?"

My sister, Laura, nods at her.

Before she tears into it, Jordan puts his hand over hers. "Can you tell everyone what it says on the envelope?"

Sara's brows furrow together in concentration as her mouth moves while she reads the words in front of her.

Smiling, she looks up at him. "It says 'for the kids'."

"Great reading, *princesa*." My chest tightens when he

speaks Spanish, the ease and love he showers my nieces and nephews with never ceasing to amaze me.

He holds his hand up, and she high fives him, before signaling for the other children, her brother Nico and my other niece and nephew, Alejandro and Lucia, to stand up. When they're all gathered around her, he gives her a quick nod. "Open it."

Sara carefully opens the seal on the envelope and stares at the contents while her brother and cousins eagerly try to see what the gift is. Her eyes widen as she pulls out what looks like a bunch of concert tickets.

"Oh my gosh," she squeals.

"What is it, *princesa?*" my mother asks.

"What are they?" Nico asks, ripping them out of her hand.

"We're going to Disneyland," she finally screams. When her words register, the other three kids echo her excitement, squealing and cheering, while eight pairs of adult eyes all turn to look at Jordan.

"Jordan," my sister, Mariana, says reprovingly.

"What?" He shrugs off her concern dismissively and rises to his feet. "I got a really good bonus at work."

Pulling another two envelopes out of his pocket, he hands one to each of my sisters. "What's this?" Mariana asks, taking it from him.

"These are the actual tickets. I just printed off Mickey Mouse cards for the kids. All the details are in there too."

"Thank you, Jordan," Laura says reverently. Rising up off the couch, she throws her arms around him and he hugs her back. "You shouldn't have."

"I wanted to," he says as my sisters switch positions and Mariana takes her turn to thank him. "And who else am I going to spend my money on? You know how much I love these kids."

Emotion and gratitude fill the room, his words a huge reminder of how important he is to this family and how important we are to him.

My dad is the first to break the heavy silence. "Okay"—he points to all the kids—"make sure you all don't forget to hug your Uncle Jordan and say thank you."

A chorus of thank yous fills the room, and the kids take turns throwing themselves at Jordan. "I'm so glad work is going well for you, *mijo*," my dad tells him proudly.

I watch his throat bob as he swallows hard, knowing how much it means to him to have my father acknowledge his hard work. As if he can feel my gaze, his eyes dart to mine, and that wistful expression from earlier crosses his face again, and for the first time in a very long time, neither of us look away.

His acts of ridiculous generosity are not unusual, but it's never anything this elaborate. And the fact that he didn't mention it to me is proof he knows a family trip to Disneyland is a little bit more than excessive.

Turning to Elena, whose head is now resting on my shoulder, I whisper, "Did you know he bought tickets for everyone?"

She gives me a quick shake of the head. "I only know what he bought you."

"Did he get me for Secret Santa?" I ask, feeling uneasy.

"So, what other presents does everyone have?" Jordan calls out, effectively ending my conversation with Elena. "Do you need any help passing out those presents?" he asks my dad.

"No, no. Mama Bear and I have it under control," he answers, using Jordan's nickname for her.

We go through the motions of my dad handing out the rest of the presents to the children, who squeal repeatedly after ripping open every one.

Thank God kids are easy to please, because after Jordan's present it would seem impossible to impress them.

When they're done, my parents recruit the grandchildren to help distribute the adults' presents, knowing that's the only way to stop them from getting too loud and too rowdy.

Years ago, we decided that we would do Secret Santa between the nine of us, picking a name out of a hat and setting a single price range for the gift, with the intention of making it less stressful and more affordable. It's a perfect solution in theory, but every year we break our own rules and there's always a present for each of us, from each of us. And as my nieces and nephews set up piles of wrapped presents for each person, I know this year isn't any different.

"Why do we even bother with Secret Santa?" Mariana asks as her son hands her all the gifts she's accumulated.

"More like why can't everyone just follow the rules?" Laura adds.

"You're both talking like you two didn't buy a slew of presents for everyone either," I chide. "Admit it. We're all as bad as each other, except maybe this year Jordan takes the cake." I shift my gaze to him as he now sits comfortably, his lap full of presents. "Way to show us up."

He glances at Elena before smirking at me. "Just wait until you see what I got you."

I turn my head to look at Elena and then back at Jordan. "What is it?"

"Nope." He shakes his head, cutting off any potential clues she could give me. "Your parents first."

Impatient but knowing he's right, I get comfortable in my seat beside Elena, who's sitting there with a shit-eating grin on her face. "Stop looking so smug," I huff jokingly. This camaraderie between them is extremely unusual; it almost feels wrong. "Your loyalty is to me."

She looks over at Jordan and then returns her gaze to mine. "It's worth it."

After a bit more ribbing, we get the children to sit back around the Christmas tree and focus our attention back to my mom and dad, who are very much used to our antics. One by one, they meticulously unwrap their presents, their faces lighting up at every gift.

There's something about spoiling my parents that brings me so much joy. Working so hard to ensure we had a roof over our heads and a stomach and fridge full of food, there was never ever any downtime for them, as they insisted on providing a life of opportunity for us.

Now that we're all older, they still work, but it's more of a hobby and to keep their minds and bodies active than a financial necessity. Their days are finally spent socializing and obsessing over their grandkids, instead of worrying about bills and hardship.

"Oh, no, no, no. You shouldn't have, it's too much," she coos, pointing at the already opened presents at her feet. "You all already bought us so much." Rising up off her chair, she extends her arms, holding the outfit we bought her in the air. "It's absolutely beautiful."

"We figured you could wear it to the wedding," Elena tells her. "I know you've got that other dress on hold, but when you tried this one—"

"You loved it, Mamá," Mariana finishes. "You deserve to feel beautiful too."

Eyes filling with tears, my mother looks around the

room, her expression full of love and adoration. "It's always too much. You're spending too much money on us."

Ignoring her, Laura gets up off the couch and reaches for the unopened box in my father's lap.

"Your turn. Open it," she says to my dad.

He adheres to her request, and a light chuckle leaves his mouth. "*Mamita*, it looks like we'll be matching."

We all laugh as he raises the tie and engraved cufflinks we all chipped in to buy him. My wedding has been all the women in my family have been able to talk about. And now that Elena and I finally agreed on a March wedding, the lead-up has turned into an exciting affair.

Knowing my parents aren't the only ones who got matching attire as gifts, I look around the room at Jordan and both of my brothers-in-law. "You guys should open your gifts too."

The three of them open the small square boxes to reveal their own stainless-steel cufflinks along with a small hand-written card. Each one of them will be standing beside me on my wedding day, and a personalized gift seemed like the perfect way to show them how much I appreciate it.

"They're engraved," I tell them.

Mariana's husband, Seth, is the first one to stand up and say thank you, clapping me on the back before kissing Elena on the cheek. Ray, Laura's husband, follows and then Jordan is standing in front of me, holding the card I wrote, his expression unreadable.

"Thanks, man," he says, an unusual amount of emotion in his voice. "You know there's nowhere else I'd rather be than standing by your side on the most important day of your life."

He glances over at Elena and gives her a soft smile, and knots form in my stomach. It's been a rocky road between them, and more than once, I've felt torn; my loyalty and love being stretched every which way.

He extends his hand to me, but basking in the possibilities of some kind of peace treaty, I take hold and pull him into me for a hug. We hold on to each other, and I let myself indulge in the fleeting moment and being this close to him without having to worry.

We're affectionate friends. This isn't unusual, but every now and then, the past creeps in and makes things feel off. Feel a little different. But instead of dwelling on feelings I've been forced to push aside, I block out the rest of the world, the background noises, and just simply hug my best friend.

3

JORDAN

RELUCTANTLY, I loosen my hold on Gael and watch him step away from me. I pretend not to hate how empty I feel without him close to me or wish that such moments we shared were more frequent.

Taking a seat beside him and Elena on the couch, my knees anxiously bounce up and down as I wait for my turn to give Gael his present. I'm not worried he's not going to like it, but after everyone's response to the Disneyland gift, I'm bracing myself for his reaction, knowing he'll think it's just a little bit too much.

When I pushed past the jealousy I have toward Elena and mentioned the idea to her, she was all on board, assuring me he would love it, and helped me realize that while he was on a break from work for the holidays was a better time for what I've got planned than closer to the actual wedding.

A part of me has to wonder if she'd still feel that way if she knew my actual motives for the extravagant and expensive gift weren't all that altruistic. I've always been jealous of her, and I was never prepared for what it would feel like to share him. It had never happened before—romantically or otherwise—and even with a proposal and wedding on the horizon, my mind and heart still find it difficult to get on board.

"Sooo," Gael draws out, pulling me out of my thoughts. "Do you want me to open your present first or you want me to give you yours?"

Perplexed, I look down at my personalized cufflinks. "I thought this was the gift."

"Don't you know you're his favorite?" Seth teases.

"Shut up," Gael retorts, nothing but humor in his voice.

We're used to it. Our friendship is always the butt of his family's jokes. They were light-hearted jibes woven with love and respect for the friendship Gael and I have. We're close. So close that there was a time his parents thought he too was gay and he and I were together.

Of course, they had no issues with it, but it was so far from the truth it was almost comical.

Almost.

The not so funny part was how I desperately wished it were that way. For as long as I can remember, he's always been the one thing I wanted. Him and me. Together.

"How about I give you my gift first?" I suggest, eager to see his reaction. "I need Seth and Ray to be here because they're in on it too."

His eyes dart between his brothers-in-law. "Is this what I think it is? You didn't, did you?"

"Did what?" I hand him an envelope much like the one I gave Sara earlier.

He holds my stare while his hands work to open it, dragging out the piece of paper I placed inside and unfolding it. As he looks down, I nervously wait for his reaction.

He lifts his head up and starts shaking it. "There's no way you're paying for all of this."

"I didn't." It's a lie, but he doesn't know that. "I told you Ray and Seth were in on it too, it's for the four of us."

The truth is, while Seth and Ray paid for their own flights, I covered the rest. And would do it a million times over just to have some time away with him.

I watch the Adam's apple in Gael's throat bob as he struggles to find the words he wants to say.

"Why don't we leave you two to it," Elena says, rising up off the couch, knowing Gael well enough that he'll need a minute to wrap his head around the gift and more than likely argue with me about how much I've spent.

Following her lead, the room empties out. With the kids already gone, all the adults unintentionally file into a line and head for the kitchen. Like the smart-ass brothers they've become to me, Seth and Ray smirk at us as they walk on by.

"Jordan," Gael says, the tone of his voice missing the reprimand and sounding more like disbelief. "This is too much."

"As your best man, I beg to differ," I counter. "It's my job to organize the bachelor party. So, I organized one."

"It didn't need to be in Vegas."

"So, you wanted it somewhere else?"

"What? No. This is *too much*," he emphasizes. "I would've been extremely happy with us starting at The Cigar Club and hitting a bar or something after. This"—he waves the piece of paper in front of my face—"is too much."

I snatch it out of his fingers. "If you don't want to go, it's fine. Seth, Ray, and I will have a great time."

He swipes the plane ticket back out of my hold. "I didn't say I didn't want to go. I just don't need a four-day bachelor party in Vegas."

He was right. He didn't need a four-day bachelor party in Vegas, but I did. I selfishly needed four uninterrupted days with my best friend before I lost him for good.

It was stupid and immature and completely nonsensical, but my head and my heart wanted it. Gael and I went to Vegas the year we both turned twenty-one, to celebrate. Ten years later, and I felt like this was a life event that deserved the same type of commemoration.

We were transitioning into a different phase of our lives, and I was viewing it as our one last hurrah before he embarked on married life with a woman who was perfect for him. It was hard to even hate Elena, because she was beautiful. Inside and out. There wasn't one reason to dislike her. Except I did, which essentially made me hate myself even more.

So, I'd invested all my wants and needs in a last-minute trip with my best friend, hoping I could finally say goodbye to the incessant ache that permanently lived in my chest because of him and wishing it would all miraculously go away the minute he and Elena exchanged those vows.

It was stupid. The smart, logical-thinking businessman part of me knew that.

But the rest of me was still, and always would be, a hopelessly devoted teenager who was and always would be, in love with his best friend.

"And for New Year's, Jordan," he adds. "This must've cost a fortune."

"Can you stop focusing on the price and get excited for your bachelor party?" I say, wanting to move on from that part of the conversation. "Plus, Elena told me because school was on winter break, you wouldn't have to ask for any vacation days."

Gael is a high school teacher. He teaches art, and he's

great at it. He's passionate in all the ways that matter—about his own art, about the process, and definitely about the students.

"You've got it all figured out, don't you?"

"Elena helped me with all the important stuff," I say honestly.

"She's a good egg," he says, and, for the first time ever, I notice the smile doesn't quite reach his eyes.

I want to ask him about the disconnect between his words and his facial expression, but I joke instead, "You're definitely punching above your weight with her."

"Fuck off." He backhands my chest. "I'm a great catch."

That you are.

"You're all right," I tease. "Now, where's my present?"

"I don't think I can give it to you after this," he says. "It's pretty lame in comparison."

I push his shoulder. "Don't be stupid. Just show me."

Striding toward the Christmas tree, he slides out a lone rectangular box wrapped in gold paper, that was half hidden behind the couch.

"Where did you get that from?"

"I hid it," he says casually. "I didn't want an audience when you opened it."

He holds it out for me upon his return.

A little giddy, I take it from him and sit down, unwrapping the paper slowly.

"Just rip it," Gael says. "It all goes in the trash anyway."

That's what he thinks. There isn't a card or sheet of wrapping paper I haven't kept since we started exchanging presents when we both turned eighteen. In a box that sits neatly in my closet, just like my feelings for him, is a lifetime of Gael and Jordan moments.

Finally, the box comes into view and I smile at the familiar logo. "You got me Monopoly?"

"I got you a personalized Monopoly board," he clarifies. "Most of the properties on there are actual properties you've sold over the years."

I look at him incredulously. "Really?"

He shrugs nonchalantly. "It's hard to buy something for the man who has everything."

A weak chuckle slips out of my mouth. If only he knew.

"Thank you," I say, feeling overwhelmed with gratitude that he is aware and attuned to my success. "You know you really didn't have to buy me a single thing."

"I wanted to," he answers. "Besides, I drew your name out of the hat anyway."

A blanket of silence settles over us, and we just stare at one another. It's been happening a lot lately. Moments where I feel like I should say something, or that he wants to tell me something. But the words never come from either of us.

"Are you guys okay in here?" Elena's voice reaches the room before she does.

On instinct, I step away from him, as if they can both read my inappropriate thoughts. "Yeah, we're good," I manage to say. "Gael's done with being ungrateful about his present."

"Shut up. You know that wasn't it." Elena sidles up beside him and he wraps an arm around her and kisses the top of her head. "I guess I'm going to Vegas."

She smiles at me, and I hate myself for being conditioned to dislike her. "Told you he'd come around eventually," she says to me. "He's just not really good at the whole receiving gifts thing. Are you, babe?"

"It's not my fault Jordan is always so over the top."

"How about we don't go over this again," I say, needing to find a space where we're not the only three people in a room. "I think I can smell your mom's pozole."

I lead the way to the kitchen, grateful to see everybody milling around the table, picking at the food and laughing.

My parents are of Eastern European descent, and while there's a whole host of traditions I had with them around the holidays, the dismissal and abandonment made it easy to leave them behind and immerse myself in those of Gael and his family.

"Jordan. *Mijo*," Gael's mom calls out. "I saved some pozole for you."

"She means she saved the whole thing for you," Mariana shouts across the room. "I wanted to go for seconds and she told me not to eat too much because there wouldn't be enough for you."

"What can I say?" I shrug, holding my hands up. "I can't help it if I'm her favorite."

"Where were you anyway?" Ray asks. "Did you get a better offer?"

That was another thing about the Herrera family traditions. You didn't usually miss them.

"He was with Frankie," Gael announces snidely, coming up behind me.

I turn to glare at him, knowing he's hitting below the belt just like I did earlier. And knowing not a single person in his family is going to let this topic go.

"You're still seeing him," Laura exclaims. "Why haven't you brought him over? Are you worried we're going to scare him away?"

A smile spreads across my face. "Of course." I gesture my arm across the room. "You'll all chew him up and spit him out."

"It's not serious," Gael tells everyone, ruining the jovial mood.

"Oh, look," Seth says. "Gael is jealous."

Both Seth and Ray laugh like two older brothers picking on the younger one. And I can't help but glance at Gael, just in time to catch the sour look on his face and Elena watching him with the same confused expression I am.

"I don't know," I say, feeling petulant and unsettled, looking directly at Gael. "Maybe after we get back from Vegas, I can bring him over."

4

———

GAEL

"ARE YOU OKAY?" Elena asks as we walk through the front door of our apartment.

We've been together for a little over two years, but we only took the leap to live together when I asked her to marry me six months ago.

Seeing that she spent most of her time at my place trying to get away from her parents anyway, it seemed like a no-brainer to ask her to move in.

It's a two-bedroom apartment in a nice quaint suburb that's not too far from the school we both work at. And it's the perfect start for two people embarking on their life together.

"You've been quiet all day," she adds.

"I'm fine," I lie, dropping our bags to the floor. "Just didn't get much sleep last night."

I'm ashamed to say it's been an adjustment. Especially on a night like tonight, where I just want the freedom to get lost in my thoughts and wallow with my deepest secrets.

"We'll be eating this food for days," she says, putting all

the leftovers my mother sent home with us into the fridge. "Do you think everyone loved their presents for the wedding?"

"Yeah," I answer absentmindedly, kicking off my shoes and sitting down on the couch. "Mom and Dad especially."

"I'm going to have a shower," she announces. I'm not even sure how she managed to be standing in front of me so quickly, but Elena begins unbuttoning her white shirt, the look in her eyes hinting ever so slightly at what her intentions are. "Do you want to join me?"

My eyes trace the length of her body, knowing how beautiful she is underneath. Over our time together, I have memorized her every curve, every dip, every taste.

But tonight, I just can't.

My face must say what my mouth is unable to articulate, and she huffs in exasperation. "I guess that's a no."

"I'm just tired," I say defensively.

"Yeah. And I'm stupid," she retorts, wrapping her shirt around her so the skin she intended to show is now well hidden.

"What's that supposed to mean?"

She waves a hand at me dismissively and stalks off to our bedroom.

"Elena," I call out, rising off the couch and following her. "Elena. Wait."

She slams the bathroom door closed. I stand there as she shuts me out, and I wonder if I really want to open this can of worms with her.

Elena and I were friends before dating. Good friends. Close friends. She knows a lot about me; things I wish she didn't.

Inhaling, I follow her into the bathroom, completely ignoring her request to be left alone.

"Elena." She freezes, standing there naked and about to step in the shower.

I reach for the back of my shirt. "What are you doing?" she asks.

"Joining you."

Leaning in, Elena switches the water off. "No, you're not."

"What? Why?"

Confidently, she places her hand on her hip, not caring that every inch of her is on display. "I don't need you to touch me because you feel bad, Gael."

"That's not what I'm doing," I protest.

She leisurely reaches for a nearby towel and wraps it around her body. "Is this about Frankie?"

God, I hated hearing that man's name. "Why are we talking about Frankie?"

"Because every time he comes up, you turn into"—she gestures her hand up and down my body—"this."

"I just don't like him for Jordan," I exclaim.

"They have sex Gael, it's hardly a marriage proposal."

"He said he would bring him over in the new year. That's more than just sex."

She shakes her head at me. "He said that because you seem to turn into an over protective, ornery father every time he mentions people he's with."

His father? God, that was so far from the truth. Nothing I felt about him was familial. Not in a long time and even less so lately.

Lately, I was fucking jealous, and Elena knew it. Every part of me knew she did, but she wasn't going to call me out. Because she was hiding from the truth just as much as I was.

"Sorry," I say, because honesty isn't really an option

right now. "I can't help but feel protective over him. Ever since—"

"I know," Elena says, nothing but understanding in her voice. "Ever since he got kicked out of his home, you've felt the need to protect him. I get it. You're the same with me," she adds with a soft smile. "You're like that with everyone you love. And we love you for it, but you need to let this disdain for Frankie go and let Jordan live his life. If it turns to shit, you'll be there for him, because that's what good friends do."

Every word she said pricked at my heart in pain, leaving little holes as reminders that this was so much more than being worried and protective of your friend. It was a lifetime of hurt, longing, lust, and confusion. And it was wrong.

Stepping closer, she places a hand on my shoulder. "Look, I'm going to have a shower and then we can continue this when I come out, if you want."

Nodding, I leave her alone in the bathroom, knowing talking is pointless. How do you tell your fiancée that she shares your heart with a man you can never have?

That you love her, but even when you shouldn't, and even when you've been pushed away, you always have, and always will love him.

By the time Elena slides into bed, I'm buried underneath the covers, willing myself to fall asleep. But Jordan returns to the forefront of my thoughts when she asks, "Were you surprised by his gift?"

Was I surprised by his gift? The financial cost of it? Yes. But by the fact that Jordan would come up with something so elaborate and inclusive? Not really.

"Did he come to you with the idea?"

"He did," she says casually. "It was awkward at first, because that's how he's always been around me."

"He has not," I argue.

"He has," she states. "Especially after you proposed."

I think back to the proposal and Jordan's shocked face when I shared the news of what I had done. He avoided me for a week, and I was sure the fact that he didn't know I was going to pop the question played a big part of it.

But I didn't even know. Sometimes life just happens and you act on instinct; my proposal to Elena was exactly that.

We weren't ones for secrets, but the more serious Elena and I became, the more Jordan and I pulled away from each other. I didn't know who had done it first, but the last six months were the most distant we'd ever been, and I hated every moment of it.

I was now engaged and he was doing whatever with Frankie, and everything that made him and me "us" has felt off ever since.

"I think it could be good for all of you," she continues. "Your sisters are trying to convince me to do some kind of bachelorette party while you're away."

I sit up, eager to no longer be the focus of the conversation. "That's a great idea. You could invite some of your friends or maybe your sisters?"

She chews on her bottom lip. "I don't know if they'd come."

Elena and her family have a complicated and toxic relationship. Two years ago, I found her crying in her car in the school parking lot after work. Not comfortable with leaving her alone in such a state, I took her out for dinner and patiently sat with her until she seemed calm enough to deal with whatever it was that had her so upset.

Turns out she was under an unbelievable amount of pressure, raising her younger twin sisters, who were under eighteen at the time, while her parents treated her like an ATM that funded their drug and alcohol addiction.

Now, both her sisters are old enough to live alone. We helped them move into Elena's old apartment when she moved in with me. But those girls, including Elena, have a lifetime of drug and alcohol exposure and abandonment issues that make it almost impossible for any of them to get along.

We both hoped the wedding would be the thing that brought her and her sisters closer, but so far it hasn't worked. My mother had wanted them to come over on Christmas Eve, but Elena and I couldn't even get them to leave the house with us.

"I know my sisters won't mind doing something low key and age appropriate if it means they'll show up," I tell her.

"I don't want to make them go through all that trouble when they probably won't come."

"There's still a few days left." I slide closer to her, wrap an arm around her shoulders, and kiss her on the head. The tension and preoccupation with Jordan now fading into the background. "I want you to have fun while I'm away. At least promise you'll consider it."

———

"OKAY. Text me when you take off and then when you land and when you get to the hotel," Elena says as she pulls up to the drop-off lane at the airport. "I don't need us to talk a million times a day, but I want to know you're safe."

Chuckling, I squeeze her hand that's resting on my thigh. "I promise to do all those things. And if you need anything, just call me. Especially if something goes down with your sisters."

"I will." Elena puts the car in park and smiles as she points out the window. "I think Seth and Ray are already drunk."

I follow the direction of her finger and see Jordan standing beside Seth and Ray, the three of them laughing with one another. It's such a familiar sight, and it sends warmth through my veins for so many different reasons.

I feel like I haven't seen Jordan laugh so freely in such a long time.

I glance back over at Elena, and I can't help but notice how sad she looks. "What is it?" I ask.

"What's what?"

"Your whole mood just changed."

She straightens. "No, it didn't."

"Hey," I say softly, reaching for her, my hand cupping her cheek. "What is it?"

She leans into me. "Promise me something."

"Anything," I say without hesitation.

"Come back to me, okay?"

Dropping my hand, it's now my turn to shift in my seat, almost like my body, as well as my mind, is trying to decipher exactly what she's saying. "I don't understand what you mean."

"I know you and Jordan…" Her voice trails off as she finds the right words. "Fuck." She rubs her hands over her face. "I've been trying to figure out how to say this for the last three days, but there is no right and perfect way to say it."

I narrow my eyes at her expectantly. "You have this unspoken connection," she states. "And every now and then I get this niggling feeling that you're not entirely over him."

I suck in a loud, long breath as the secrets I told her during the development of our friendship are regurgitated to mean something completely different now that she's my fiancée.

"I trust you," she says. "I really do. But please. Please come back to me."

5

JORDAN

AFTER A SMOOTH FLIGHT FROM SEATTLE, the four of us are standing in the extravagant foyer of the Aria. It's opulent, yet sleek in its design. Lots of browns and blacks and silvers with a pop of color hanging from the ceiling and a sporadic dash of greenery decorating the lobby.

It doesn't have the extreme glitz of Caesars Palace or The Bellagio, but it's a huge step up from the first time Gael and I visited Las Vegas. The first and only time we visited, we were both still studying and had saved for ages to be able to afford the trip. We stayed at the Rio, off the Strip, and spent all our time at the casino and club hopping, only returning to the not-so-glitzy hotel to sleep.

Standing in the check-in line, the four of us are huddled closely together, holding our suitcases; Ray and Seth look like two kids in a candy store, both of them taking photos like true tourists. I wouldn't say they don't get out much, but the anticipation of having a guys' only weekend away was written all over their faces.

Vegas is intoxicating. It didn't matter if it was your first time or your hundredth time, the thrill and the adrenaline never waned. Add in the hype that surrounded New Year's and it was almost impossible not to get swept up in the excitement.

Just as we move closer to the check-in desk, my phone vibrates in my pocket. There's only one person I'm really expecting to call, so I drag my phone out of my back pocket and subtly give Gael my back while answering.

"Hey," I greet.

"Hey," the voice on the other end answers. "Have you guys checked in?"

"Not yet. We're still in the line."

"Deacon and I just finished lunch, and we were going to head back to the room for a bit, but if you want us to come down now, we can."

We shuffle a bit farther forward while I'm on the phone, so I pull the cell away from my ear and check the time.

"We'll be checking in soon. How about I give you our room number as soon as I get it and you both meet us there?"

"That sounds great. I'll wait for your text."

Hanging up, I turn and find Gael looking at me expectantly. "What?" I ask, playing dumb.

"Who's here?"

"Just let the surprise play out, yeah?"

Huffing, he faces the front, neither of us saying a word till we make it to the check-in desk. Dragging my driver's license out of my wallet, I hand it to the concierge. "I've got a reservation under the name Jordan Varga."

Offering me a smile and a soft nod, she taps away at her computer before printing off some paperwork and scanning the plastic cards over the machine that activates them.

"Okay, Mr. Varga, here are your room keys." She slides

them over the marble counter in a cardboard sleeve. "You've got the two-bedroom Sky Suite; each room has two double beds and its own en suite bathroom."

"Jordan," Gael pipes in.

Knowing very well he's going to bring up the price, *again*, I wordlessly hand him the room keys and hope it's enough to shut down his inevitable protest. Obliging, he passes them on to Ray and Seth and then slides his own in his front pocket.

"Jordan," Gael repeats. Ignoring him, I follow Seth and Ray to the bank of elevators while Gael follows me. "I know you can hear me," he continues. "Promise me you're done with the extravagant spending."

Knowing he can't see me, I roll my eyes, wanting to petulantly argue that I can do whatever the fuck I want with my money, but I know it's pointless. We have this argument often, and while to outsiders it may look like I'm being ostentatious and he's either intimidated or ungrateful, it's actually neither.

Early on, Gael worked out that I use my money to "pay off" my debt to him and his family for all they've done for me. He hates it, but I don't plan on changing it.

Not now. Not ever, and I don't want to dampen our time away too early. Instead, I text our mystery guests our room number and follow the others to our room in silence.

The walk from the elevator isn't too long, and when Seth opens the door and steps inside, he lets out a low, impressed whistle before turning to face me.

"You did good, bro," he compliments. "This is fucking amazing."

Both Gael and Ray agree as we all pass the threshold and move farther into the room. We're standing in the living area, taking in the view of the Strip that spans the length of the suite.

On one side is a kitchen and communal bathroom, and on the other are two doors that lead to either bedroom. The room is decorated in dark colors, pops of silver and white scattered across the large backdrop of black and glass furniture. It's refined and polished, almost giving off an elite gentlemen's club feel.

"I'm going to FaceTime Mariana and give her a tour of the place," Seth says, interrupting my perusal. "She's gonna fucking hate me."

The smile on his face is a complete contradiction to the words he says. In fact, I'm almost certain he's eager to tease his wife.

"I'm going to do the same," Ray chimes in. And when I look at Gael, he too is pulling his phone out.

"I'm just going to dump my bag in the room," I say, trying hard not to pout about how obviously single I am right now. Rushing to the room, I close the door and gladly hide away from all the love and romance that I stupidly didn't anticipate.

Because I always unpack, no matter how short the stay, I rest my small suitcase on the bed and begin to separate my clothes and toiletries. Just as I finish hanging up a few dress shirts, Gael walks in with his duffel in hand.

"Hey," Gael greets.

"Hey, what did Elena think of the room?" I ask.

"She loved it, obviously. Totally jealous. I'm sure she and Mariana and Laura will be bitching up a storm tonight in a three-way conversation."

"I'm glad to have provided some entertainment for you all."

He drops his bag to the bed and lets himself fall back on it. "Want to unpack my bag?"

"No fucking chance," I say with a small chuckle.

"Thought I'd give it a try."

My cell pings, and I watch Gael get up with a renewed enthusiasm and try to swipe it off my bed.

"No, you don't," I say, snatching it out of his grip.

Huffing, he lies back on the bed. "I hate when you're so cagey."

"Let me enjoy it a little," I gloat. "It's hard to keep shit from you anyway."

Looking down at the screen, I swipe at the notification and quickly reply to the text. "If you want to open the hotel door, the surprise is on the other side," I inform him.

Too excited, he doesn't bother to wait for me, and I listen for the sound of surprised voices before I leave the room and join them.

At the sound of the bedroom door clicking, Gael turns around, the smile he wears splitting his face. "I can't believe you got Julian and Deacon here without me knowing."

I shove my hands in my pockets and walk toward them. "You need to start giving me credit for the secrets I keep."

The statement is supposed to be a lighthearted retort, but the layers of truth about just how deep my secrets run resonates and ruminates in my head for way too long.

When I reach them, Julian extends his hand out, and I take it, bringing him in for a hug. "How have you been, man?"

"It's been good," he responds, clapping me on the back. "Deacon and I thought we'd squeeze in a bit more alone time and spend Christmas here without the family."

Turning to Deacon, I offer my hand in greeting. "It's

good to see you again. I appreciate you guys making the time to come."

Julian and Gael met when Julian started working at Greensday High. They hit it off immediately, Gael eventually introducing me into the fold and Julian doing the same with Deacon. They were the kind of guys that you didn't need to live in their pockets for them to be there for you when you needed them to be.

"Are you kidding?" Julian says. "I wouldn't miss celebrating with you guys for the world. But I won't lie, the fact that I get to spend uninterrupted days with my husband definitely sealed the deal." As if the word "husband" summoned Deacon, he moves closer, throwing his arm over Julian's shoulder and kissing him on the temple.

Automatically, I turn my head away from the blatant display of affection, my chest full of yearning.

Despite the breakdown of my relationship with my parents when I told them I was gay, I was as traditional and family oriented as they come.

I wanted what Julian and Deacon had. I wanted it with Gael, and that was the part I hated wanting.

"Are you listening?" Gael's voice pierces through my self-destructive thoughts.

"Sorry, what?" I shake my head. "I didn't hear you."

"Are we going to start drinking?"

"Yes. Of course." I clap my hands together a little too enthusiastically. "Let's get this show on the road."

6

———

GAEL

IN ONE OF the hotel bars, the six of us are sitting around a large table, Ray and Seth in a deep discussion about gambling and whether it's all based on skill or luck. I tune them out while listening to Julian and Deacon and also trying to work out what's up with my best friend.

For someone who organized the time away, I expected him to be a little bit more enthusiastic, but the whole ordeal is feeling more like a chore than something he wanted to participate in.

When I notice Deacon's eyes covertly looking at him, I know I'm not the only one who's noticed his mood.

"Hey." I gently elbow him. "Everything okay?"

"Shit." He shakes his head, as if to rid himself of whatever thoughts are plaguing him. When he notices the whole table looking at him, he stands hastily. "Sorry. Let me go and get another round."

"I'll come with you," Deacon says.

Both Julian and I watch them leave, and when I finally drag my gaze off his retreating body, I notice Ray and Seth have left the table too.

"Where did they go?" I ask, feeling out of my element.

"I think they're leaving the drinking to us while they cover the gambling portion of the trip," he explains with a soft chuckle. "So, this was nice of Jordan to organize."

"You could've told me."

"And have him kick my ass? Yeah, no thanks."

I look over in the direction Jordan went and then back to Julian. "He's being weird, isn't he?"

"A little," he says honestly. "Did something happen?"

"I don't know." I shrug. "If I'm honest, he's been off for a while."

I want to correct myself and say *we've* been off for a while, but I don't. "He was fine on the plane. The four of us were talking and laughing like normal, but when we got into the room, his mood just flipped."

A moment of silence passes between us, Julian picking at the label on his beer bottle.

"What?" I ask.

"Nothing," he says, lowering his gaze back to his drink.

Annoyed, I pull the bottle out of his grasp, and he looks up at me in confusion.

"I know you have something to say, so tell me," I insist.

"Every time I bring it up, you brush it off, so I'm not going to."

"You think he's in love with me," I say, repeating the words Julian has said to me since the first time he met Jordan.

"You know he is," he says with conviction, and I don't bother arguing, because I feel like I've known it for a long time. Maybe even wanted it to be true. "And all things considered, maybe watching you get ready for your wedding is a little hard on him."

"I didn't ask him to do all this," I say guiltily.

Julian sighs. "He can still hurt and want to make you happy."

I sit there, refusing to look at my friend or further discuss his theories. It's not a door I want to open right now, and definitely not with Julian. The only person I would dare to breathe life into the possibility with is Jordan himself. And no matter how badly I want him to, he's always been too scared to open up that door with me.

Hearing Jordan laugh, I turn to see him and Deacon returning with our drinks, internally thanking Deacon for whatever they talked about to make his mood considerably brighter. His eyes catch mine, and he smiles at me. It's not apologetic or forced, but it's the one that has *always* assured me that everything's going to be okay.

I return the gesture and push away the concern that was consuming me earlier. For now, I'm not a mind reader, and I'm not going to worry. If something is wrong with Jordan, I have to trust he'll find the time to tell me.

Conversation resumes, flowing without even the slightest hiccup, as if Jordan's bad mood was a figment of my imagination. We continue to add to our drink count, and by the time Seth and Ray return, the six of us have all passed the buzzed stage and are firmly in the drunk zone.

I feel light and carefree, the tension I've been carrying for so long, slowly but surely dissipating. Between the stresses of Christmas and the wedding, Elena and her family, and Elena and Jordan, this time away with friends is exactly what I needed.

Standing, Seth and Ray both finish off their drinks and then signal to the Casino floor. "You guys coming this time?"

"What are you playing?" Deacon asks.

"We'll probably find a poker table," Seth answers. "And hunker down for a long night."

"I'd rather not play," Deacon says, glancing at Julian. "I don't want to commit to anything, in case I get a better offer."

They share a smile, the love and adoration they have for one another unmissable. Deacon looks at Julian like he's the sun, and it's hard to imagine a time where these two men didn't get along.

Julian's told me the story so many times, how he was with Deacon's brother before he died, and Deacon had never been with another man before him. It was heartbreaking and romantic and a little reminder that just because it isn't always easy, it doesn't mean it isn't going to work out.

I subtly glance at Jordan who's also watching Deacon and Julian. He wants what they have. The yearning is written all over his face.

You would think commitment and attachment would be foreign and unappealing to Jordan after what his parents did to him, but he has never shied away from admitting he wants that domestic life. He wants a life and a future that he's created with people that he chose and who chose him in return.

The house. The husband. The kids.

In a perfect world, I could be the one to give those things to him.

I glance away quickly, wanting to dismiss the life-changing thought and focus on the truer part of the sentiment. Jordan does deserve to have what he wants. He does deserve to have all the love in the world and then some. Someone to hold him and cherish him. Someone to protect him and be the family he so desperately wants for himself.

Intoxicated and clearly feeling a little ballsy, Jordan looks directly at me. "How about we try a game of roulette?"

"Sure. I love that game," I deadpan, and I can almost see the words "I know" sitting on the tip of his tongue, but instead, he just nods at me nonchalantly, pretending he didn't reference something we've ignored since we were twenty-one.

"Let's find a table," I say. "Is anyone going to join?"

"We'll join you for a bit," Julian supplies.

"Seth? Ray?"

"We'll meet you there later," Seth tells me. "If we get caught up playing poker, we'll just meet you guys back at the room."

"Sounds good."

The two of them leave the table while the four of us walk in the opposite direction in search of an empty-looking roulette table.

"Jordan," Julian says. "What else did you plan this weekend?"

He glances at me before returning his focus to Julian. "I figured we'd see what Gael wants to do, but I did schedule for us to have dinner on New Year's Eve before going out, and for all of us to do that supercar driving experience the day after."

"The one we wanted to do last time we were here?" I ask, interrupting him.

"Yeah." He rubs a hand over the back of his neck nervously. "I figured since we didn't get to, and we'd all get a kick from racing the cars, it'd be a good idea."

"Fuck yeah," Deacon, who lives and breathes cars, shouts excitedly. "My best friend, Wade, and I did it a while back, and I can only imagine it's even better now. It was such a rush."

Jordan and I grew up watching all the *Fast and the Furious* movies and spending endless amount of hours battling it out for the top spot while playing *Grand Theft Auto* and *Formula One*. Our infatuation with racing has me giddy at what he's planned.

Knowing how much thought Jordan has put into this, I can't help but feel the need to be close to him. I speed up my steps and sidle up next to him, throwing my arm over his shoulders and dropping a lazy, drunken kiss on his cheek. "Thank you."

His face softens, a languid smile stretches across his face, losing the tension he's been walking around with all day. "Anything for you, you know that."

Reluctantly, I untangle myself from him, but we continue our search for a roulette table in silence, and I pray the awkwardness is well behind us now.

When we find what we're looking for, Jordan and I spend a few minutes explaining the rules to Julian and Deacon, who seem more interested in being spectators and cheering us on than playing.

After ordering a round of shots and beers as chasers, Jordan and I decide to pool our money together. I hand over the cash to the dealer, and he slides five black chips over the felt table in our direction.

"Place your bets," the dealer calls out, and Jordan reaches over me and places one round disc on a black eleven before taking possession of the rest of the chips. It's the exact same play I would've chosen. With both our birthdays falling on the eleventh day of the month, it's been our lucky number for as long as I can remember.

The dealer follows up with a "no more bets," and the

table falls into a muffled silence as we all watch and wait with bated breath as he spins the wheel.

A disappointed "fuck" leaves Jordan's mouth as the little white ball stops on a red twenty-five, but that doesn't stop him from placing another hundred dollars on the same exact square.

I look over my shoulder. "Are you sure?"

"When has this number ever steered us wrong?"

I swallow hard, trying my best not to conjure up the memory of a moment so very similar to this one. When we lose another three times, I watch him place the last hundred-dollar chip down with nothing but absolute certainty and confidence that we've got this.

He nudges my shoulder. "Don't look so disheartened, you know this is our hand."

"I'm not going to watch," I tell him, my stomach rolling in nerves. I'm not a huge gambler, and my mind always spends money like a struggling college student, constantly forgetting I have more than I had then and I can afford to splurge on whatever I want every now and then.

"Come on," he cajoles. He wraps an arm around my neck, keeping me in place. "Watch us win our money back."

Chewing on my bottom lip, I anxiously wait for the wheel to stop spinning. When the ball lands on a black eleven, I hear Julian and Deacon cheering in excitement behind us and Jordan just squeezes my shoulder.

It's the simplest action, but it sobers me up immediately, bringing every suppressed memory to the surface. I turn to look at him, and his eyes are already on me. Staring at one another, I let myself revisit my most painful memory, remembering the screaming and cheering. Remembering the adrenaline and the excitement of being two young, drunk kids winning a shitload of money and feeling on top of the world.

Remembering the way he wrapped me in his arms.

Remembering the way he pressed his lips to mine.

Remembering how much I wanted it.

Jordan's gaze drops down to my lips, the alcohol and Vegas making him obvious and reckless, and I know he's right there next to me on this trip down memory lane.

My heart pounds almost painfully. It's been ten years, and there hasn't been a day that's passed that I haven't thought of our one and only kiss.

The way he felt.

The way I felt.

The perfection of it all.

But he pushed me away. He didn't want it, didn't want me. And I didn't realize until this very moment how much I'd never really gotten over the pain from his rejection.

Our friendship survived, because it means everything to me. *He* means everything to me.

Losing Jordan would be like losing a limb, and no matter how much I wanted to explore more with him, I was too scared to rock the boat. The rejection already left a scar, and I couldn't deal with the devastation of jeopardizing that soul-deep attachment I had to him.

Needing air, I shift out from under his arm and bump into a confused looking Deacon and Julian. Not wanting to talk to any of them, I let the panic and adrenaline control my movements, turning away and pushing my body forward as my legs take me across the casino floor and to the bank of elevators.

I don't look back.

I can hear them all calling my name, but I don't give in to the temptation, because there's no way I want to process any of this with an audience. And I sure as hell don't want to hear Jordan deny what just passed between us.

There's no way I'm going to confess to him in the middle of the casino floor how much that moment hurt, or that he broke my heart. Or even worse, admit that I'm marrying someone else, even though I never really got over it. Got over him.

7

—————

GAEL

I TEAR through the hotel suite and fly into our shared room, hating that there's no way for me to put distance between us. Slamming the door, I fall like a heap of limbs onto the floor and press my back to the door, my chest heaving.

Burying my head in my hands, I let the helplessness and hopelessness of the situation overwhelm me.

I try to channel my thoughts into Elena.

Come back to me.

We're supposed to have a future together.

Come back to me.

I try to envision our upcoming wedding and reminisce on all the best parts of our relationship, but the cracks I've so desperately tried to patch up resurface, and just like weeds, my insecurities and betrayal seep through the perfect picture I've tried so hard to create.

But it's all useless. Futile. Because Jordan's there. In every memory. Every feeling. It was him first, and shamefully, I knew everything else was just second best.

Come back to me.

I feel my chest cracking right down the middle. Right and wrong. Past and present. Him and her.

It isn't supposed to be like this. This confusing. This complicated.

I had too much love to give to a man who didn't know what to do with it, when there was a beautiful woman, wanting my whole heart, sitting at home alone, waiting for me.

Come back to me.

Just like I expected, it's been less than five minutes and there's already a harsh, hurried knock on the door. "Gael," Jordan calls out. I ignore him and he knocks again. "Gael. Please. I need you to open up. I need to talk to you."

Swallowing hard, I push past the wedge of emotions stuck in my throat. "I can't."

"Please," he begs, and the painful crack in his voice cinches itself around my heart. "It's me. Please."

Resigned, I hear him slide his body down the wooden door, and I assume he's sitting the exact same way I am. After a minute or two, I hear his voice close to my ear.

"Tell me why you ran."

Even though I know he can't see me, I still shake my head. "Don't act like you don't know."

"It doesn't mean I don't want to hear it."

Placing my hand on the door, I turn my body, as if the shift in positions will change the distance between us, and mull over the possibility of finally being honest with Jordan. What that will mean for him and for me, and for Elena.

After years of ignoring that kiss, am I finally ready to open up this can of worms? Can I really hear how, even after all this time, and all the feelings I have bottled up, he still wants every other man but me?

"You broke my heart, Jordan." My voice trembles, but

the surprising sliver of instant relief I feel at uttering those few words gives me the courage I need to continue. "I wanted that kiss so badly, and I let you convince me that I didn't." I think back to the heated conversation we had after. I think back to all the times I've wanted to kiss him ever since. "I'd never kissed another guy or wanted to. So, yeah, maybe I was a little confused about my sexuality, but I wasn't confused about you. *I wasn't*," I repeat, driving that single, most important point home, hoping he understands what I'm trying to say.

"I let you convince me that you knew better. I let you convince me that I was mistaking our friendship for something more. And we were close. We *are* close," I correct. "So I let myself believe you. Told myself you were right, and that *I* was the one who had my wires crossed, because if I didn't, it meant..." I take a deep breath before revealing the one possibility that hurts the most. "It meant that you didn't want me."

"Gael," he says hoarsely.

Ignoring him, I continue, not wanting to lose my nerve, needing to get it all out, consequences be damned, because I couldn't carry this any longer.

I couldn't hold in the lie, and I deserved to know the truth. We both did.

"But I've seen it, Jordan. Through all the years, I've fucking seen how you've watched me when you think I'm not looking. I've seen how much you wanted me."

"Elena," he says with a choked whisper.

"You think I don't fucking know that?" I scream. Turning around to face the door, I slam my fist against the wood in fury. "You think I don't fucking know how much I'm hurting her; how much is at risk with every word that leaves my mouth right now?"

"Then don't do it," he shouts back. "Forget about it all. Forget about this conversation. Forget about the kiss. She's your future, Gael."

Unrestrained anger bubbles through me at his words.

Forget about it? If I could've, I would have.

"Forget about it," I bellow, rising to my feet and aggressively swinging the door open.

I don't know what I expect to see on the other side, but Jordan running his hand over the back of his neck, nervously looking over at me with so much hurt and pain in his blue eyes, has me swallowing back my argument.

"You don't really want me," he starts. His voice is soft and lacks conviction, but he continues anyway. "You're not gay, you're not into guys. You never were. You're not."

My anger bubbles up to the surface.

"You think I fucking care about labels?" I scoff, fuming at his repeated dismissal. "Why do you do this? Why do you always try to talk me out of my feelings for you? Why don't you fucking believe me?"

He exhales loudly and then closes the distance between us, slamming the door behind him and pushing us farther into the room. Toe-to-toe, he uncharacteristically cradles my head in his hands. His tender touch softening me. "Because I won't survive having you and losing you," he says in a shaky breath. "To wake up one day and have you realize it wasn't what you thought it would be or that it was the chase that you actually enjoyed. That I was just an experiment or a momentary lapse in judgment." He shakes his head, his Adam's apple bobbing in his throat. "My heart can't take that, Gael."

Winded by his painful truth and his fear, I lose the hostility and find my courage, mirroring his actions. My palms brushing against the scruff of his cheeks, my eyes never leaving his. "And what about me? Don't I get a say in this? Don't I get to say how *I* feel? Or tell you what my heart can take?"

My heart rattles in my chest as I lay it all on the line. The close proximity of his body to mine, our hands touching one another, the words leaving our lips.

A conversation with him is everything I've ever wanted, but fear consumes me. I am playing with fire; my feelings and actions in this moment have the power to delight or destroy more than the two of us in this room.

"I can't do this with you," he says, averting his gaze from mine, his hands dropping away from my face. "You're getting married to someone else."

The lines between right and wrong, and saying too much and not enough, are blurring. And I have never felt so powerless in my life. Powerless to my thoughts. To my heart. To him.

"If you want this with me, Jordan…" Strong and unwavering, the words leave my mouth without a single care for the consequences. "I'll do anything to be with you."

Jordan's breath hitches at my confession.

"I've waited for years for you to tell me," I continue, as if now I've opened the floodgates, the words just can't stop. "I've waited for you to be the one to break the silence and bring your feelings up to me." I skim my thumb across his cheekbone, the intimate touch foreign but welcome, and I want nothing more than to be able to touch him like this, always. "I almost thought I was imagining it," I add. "Like I'd made it all up in my head."

"Almost?" He hedges.

Swallowing hard, I keep his gaze locked on mine, giving him no room, making sure there's no space between us. "Sometimes, I'd catch you looking at me. And that look… I knew that look. I knew it, because I felt it." My hands fall away from his face, and I reach out to clasp his. Raising them to my chest, I place his palms over my heart. "Here," I say, adding pressure to my hands, ensuring he can feel the strong rhythm of my heartbeat. "I felt it here. Every. Single. Time."

He drops his head to my shoulder, as if he's struggling to process all the emotions. His and mine.

"Please, Jordan," I whisper, my voice strangled, losing its confidence, worried that I've just split my heart open for nothing. "Talk to me. Tell me this isn't all in my head."

"Why are you marrying Elena?" I don't know why I didn't expect this question, but I can feel the myriad of emotions crossing my face as I try to think of the right answer. We're past the point of lying, and I'm past the point of redemption.

All I have is my heart and my words and my honesty, and I hope that in the end it's enough.

"I love her."

8

————

JORDAN

HE LOVES HER.

My body stiffens at his admission, and Gael feels it. The three words are simple, honest, and so fucking obvious, because of course he loves her.

"It's a good thing you're marrying her, then," I say flatly, mildly impressed I'm able to keep the snark and hurt out of my voice.

Confused and needing space—needing to nurse my already bruised and battered heart—I push at his solid chest and try to step out of his hold. But he doesn't budge.

He effortlessly moves his hands to my hips, as if we've always touched each other like this, and his fingers press into me, holding me still. Holding me close, making sure I don't walk away.

"Let me go," I say, the demand weak on my lips.

"No."

"Gael," I breathe out. "Please."

He shakes his head, and even though every fiber of my being knows how dangerous this is, being like this, I stay still. I stand there and let him hold me, intimately, as he tells me he loves somebody else.

Slowly, his hands rise, ghosting the length of me and settling on either side of my neck. "Ask me why I'm not with you. Why I'm not marrying you."

Unable to look at him, I turn my head, and he persists with the questioning. "Ask me why, Jordan."

"Stop," I plead. Forcefully, I step out of his hold and let my eyes land on his. "What is the point, Gael?" I ask, exasperated. "What is the fucking point of rehashing all the things we want and can't have?"

"Why can't we have them?" he says.

I scoff. "Am I missing something here? You just said you're marrying Elena because you love her."

"I also said I would do anything to be with you," he counters.

Did he really mean what he said?

My head is spinning at his words. I feel like I'm living in a parallel universe, or I'm dreaming and my brain still can't work out if this is the best dream I've ever had or if it's going to turn into my worst fucking nightmare.

Fear paralyzes me, and my tongue thickens in my mouth, every part of me torn between running to him or running away from this.

"Okay, then," I concede, shoving my hands into my pockets. "Why aren't you marrying me?"

He raises his hand in defeat and shrugs. "Because for some ridiculous reason, you won't let me love you."

"No." I shake my head in disagreement, beginning to pace across the length of the hotel room. It isn't that simple. There's no way it is *that* simple. "No, Gael. That's not it."

"You know I was in love with you before we kissed, right?"

My feet falter, and I stop to look at him. He's now leaning against the closed door, as if he doesn't have a care in the world, his arms crossed over his chest, accentuating his perfectly sculpted body. *God, he's so fucking beautiful.*

With his tanned skin, jet-black hair, thick and long eyelashes that brighten his chestnut-colored eyes, he's always been the man I compare every other one to.

He looks so relaxed, so comfortable with every single revelation, and it has me wondering if it is that simple. If over the years I made up every reason why it would never work between us.

If I'm really the *only* reason we're not together.

"I'm not going to lie," he adds. "For a while, I was worried if I was confusing our friendship for love, or whether I was letting all the jokes about us being secretly in love get to me. And I'd only been with girls."

"Have you been with other guys?" I blurt out, wondering if this is a side of him he's kept from me.

He shakes his head, and every part of me deflates, not understanding why he's so sure of himself, even though he's never been with any other men.

As if he can read my thoughts, he pushes off the door and stalks toward me, shaking his head. "Don't," he warns.

"Don't what?"

"Don't reduce what's between us to our sexual experiences. This isn't about who we've been with, this is just about realizing we're right for one another."

"And when you realize dick isn't for you?" I sneer.

Triggered by my retort, he strides over to me in three easy steps and pushes me up against the wall behind me. His hands are placed on either side of my face, his breath warm, and his eyes wide with determination. "Don't confuse my lack of experience for lack of understanding. I know what I want. I know who I am. I know what matters, and I know what doesn't. The only thing that you need to know is, being attracted to other men doesn't change a single thing, because it's only ever been you."

"So, the only man you want to be with is me, but you could replace me with a woman?"

He drops his hands and then runs them through his curly head of hair. "That's so far from the truth and you know it. And what about all the men you jump into bed with? Huh?" he challenges. "So, you can replace me, and I can't do the same?"

"I'm not marrying any of them," I spit out. "We both know it's not the same thing. I'm not promising forever and a future, I'm just fucking them."

As if I've slapped him, he retreats from my words, walking backward until the back of his knees hit the edge of the bed. Dropping to the mattress, he buries his head in his hands before finally looking up at me.

"She was pregnant." The words are nothing more than a soft murmur, but I hear them loud and clear.

"What?" I'm completely stunned, because that's not at all what I expected. I just stare at him. Dumbfounded. "When?"

"I proposed because she was pregnant," he explains. "And then she miscarried, and I wasn't going to take it back."

Switching gears, I shift from the heartbroken best friend to the supportive one, wondering how much more we've been keeping from each other. Moving in his direction, I take a seat beside him on the bed. "Why didn't you tell me?"

"You would've talked me out of marrying her," he says. "You would've told me I could be a good enough dad without tying myself to someone I wasn't sure about."

With no time to process each revelation, I focus on one thing at a time. "You would've been right," I tell him. "Married or not, there's no way you would be anything but the best dad, Gael."

"Maybe." He shrugs. "But we both know there are some hard limits my family has, and having a baby out of wedlock is one of them."

Gael's family lived and breathed Catholicism. Add in the heavy influence of Mexican culture, and they had some strict views on marriage, children, and family.

It came as such a shock to me that they never even thought twice about letting me find refuge in their home. They never lectured me about my sexuality or even hinted that it bothered them, so it always surprised me to hear them voice their rigid expectations to Gael and his sisters.

"Okay." I drag the word out as my mind tries to sensitively put my next sentence together. "And the miscarriage? Are you okay? Is Elena okay?"

Gael squeezes his eyes shut at my question, and I know I've just tapped into something so much more than what's going on between me and him. Guilt eats at me for not knowing what he was going through, for not being there for him.

"I know why they say people have babies to fix their problems," he says. "Because in those few weeks, everything was perfect. I could imagine that life for us."

My chest tightens with jealousy at his honesty, but I do my best to ignore the pain. "And now?" I brace myself for an explanation as to why they're still getting married, but he doesn't say a word. "So where does that leave you two now? You obviously love her enough to give it a go. To stay?"

"I love her enough," he echoes. "I love her enough to not want to hurt her."

He turns his head to look at me, his big, beautiful brown eyes sad and honest, the conviction and confidence from earlier no longer visible. "But I also love her enough to be honest with her."

I want to be mad that he's waited this long to tell me. I want to be mad he's waited this long to be honest with Elena. I want to be mad he's put himself in this impossible situation, where he looks like the bad guy, and he's anything but.

The truth is, the only person I should be mad at is me.

But I was too wrapped up in protecting myself, I didn't see what was probably right in front of me. Not about Gael and me and not about Gael and Elena.

I was scared... I'm *still* scared.

Taking a deep breath, I muster courage I didn't even know I had and finally ask the unavoidable questions. "Does she know how you feel about me?"

"She knows some of it."

His answer surprises me. "What did you tell her?"

"One day she mentioned how close we were and asked if I knew you were into me." My cheeks heat at the realization that the one thing I thought was a well-kept secret, wasn't a secret at all. "I told her I knew you were into me at one stage of your life and that we'd kissed once."

He runs both hands over his face before turning his whole body to face me. "I told her the kiss changed me. I told her it opened my eyes. Showed me I might've been in love with you, and that I probably had been for a lot longer than I realized."

I notice he doesn't use the word loved. It's all present tense, and that flicker of hope I've been desperately trying to extinguish returns. "What did she say to that?" I ask, my voice low and almost shy.

"We were friends. And she did nothing but listen when I told her it didn't matter, because you didn't love me back."

It's on the tip of my tongue to tell him that's not the truth, to tell him how much I really do love him. To tell him I loved him before I even knew what the word meant, before I even really understood what the feelings I'd felt for him for so long really meant. But instead, I delve deeper, asking questions I don't even want the answers to.

"And that explanation... that was enough for her?"

"If it wasn't, she never said anything," he states. "She and I..." He takes a deep breath. "We're not perfect. I am *not* perfect, but we're honest with one another."

They do seem to be more transparent than he and I have ever been, but I hear and feel his dig all the same.

Unable to meet his gaze, I rub my hands up and down my thighs and concentrate on the repetitive motion, hoping it calms me. I don't know where we're supposed to go from here, but I know there's no way I'll be able to forget everything he's said to me. The way he feels. About me. About us.

All the possibilities.

"I can't go back," I whisper, and it's the most honest I've been with him and myself since we came back to the room. "I don't know what any of this means, but I can't forget everything you've just told me."

Seemingly annoyed by our distance, he rises up off the bed and crouches between my spread legs. He places his hands on mine and patiently waits till my eyes find his.

"I don't want you to go anywhere, Jordan. Just be *here*. With me."

I look down at our clasped hands and back up at him. "I don't know if I can. Not while you're still with her."

It's a weak excuse, because it doesn't feel like morals

and ethics have a place here. Well, they don't for me, even if that does make me sound like a piece of shit. Because the truth is, Gael being with Elena isn't the whole issue. It's the worry that we'll have this time together and then he'll go back to her. That fear of losing him is so much greater than the joy of having him, so I hold on to that reasoning like a lifeline, to save myself from the heartache I know I'll never recover from.

I don't want to hurt her, or ruin his life, but the layers of complexity that surround us feel so much bigger than a relationship that seems to ooze more convenience than compatibility.

Clearing my throat, I thread my fingers through his and give them a little squeeze. "Why don't you go downstairs with Deacon and Julian and I'll be down soon."

A humorless laugh leaves his mouth. "No, you won't."

I almost want to smile, because he's right, but I persevere. "Look," I say a little too harshly. "I just need to process this, okay?"

Frustrated, he stands up, and my gaze follows. "Which part do you need to process?" he shouts, throwing his hands in the air. "The part where I tell you over and over that I want you, or the part where you keep telling me that I don't?"

"I don't fucking know," I shout, matching his frustration. "I don't fucking know."

In a split moment of weakness or strength—I can't decide which—Gael is back up in my space, standing between my legs and forcing me to fall back on the mattress as I look up at him.

Long gone is the placid, rational man; a hungry and hurt man in his place. His eyes blaze with desire and determination, and my body thrums at the way his attention is all mine. It's been ten years since we skirted around the edges of possibility, and as he raises a knee to the bed and hovers over me, I know there will be no turning back after this.

If I let him touch me, there won't be another ten years of fear and indecision. It can only be all or nothing. And whichever way it goes, I know I won't ever recover.

Gael's mouth descends to mine, and I want to cry from the sheer perfection of feeling his lips pressed to mine. Pulling back, his gaze flickers between my mouth and my eyes. "What don't you know?" he asks, his voice a throaty whisper. "More importantly, *how* don't you know?"

My brain short circuits when he moves to kiss me again, and the last words to leave his lips reverberate in my head, because he's right, *how don't I know?*

Instinctively, I raise my hands to his hips, gripping him tight and holding him right where I want him. With purpose, his mouth moves against mine, and I try to catalog every motion, every taste. I tell myself to savor the moment, but when his tongue sweeps across the seam of my lips, my self-restraint slips.

"Don't stop," I breathe out.

And he doesn't. With focus and certainty, Gael kisses me, like he hasn't stopped kissing me for the last ten years. He kisses me like this isn't new. He kisses me like I'm not the first and only man he's been with. He kisses me with promise. He kisses me with pride.

He kisses me like he loves me.

Needing more, I slip my hands underneath his shirt, and my skin tingles at the contact. I run my fingertips up and down the sides of his body, loving the goose bumps that I leave in my wake.

The thought of being able to touch him like this sends

every part of me into overdrive, my cock thickening in my pants, and my mind reeling that this is *finally* happening.

I'm enamored by his ease, and when I drag him down to lay on top of me, I'm elated at the way his hard length grazes against my own.

"You're hard," I murmur, the surprise evident in my voice. A mixture of disbelief that I'm not dreaming and relief that his body wants me just as much as his heart and his mind do.

Raising his head to look at me, Gael rests on his forearms and chuckles. "Are you telling me all I had to do was show you I could get hard for you and you would believe me?"

I try to hide my smile, but it's futile. "It's kind of hard to fake, that's all."

"Because I'm not faking it," he retorts, a little less humor in his voice.

I lift my hand to his face and trail my fingers across his cheekbone and down his jaw. "It feels surreal to be touching you like this," I admit, knowing, even though nothing feels concrete, I can't turn him away from me now. Not when, in this moment, in this room, we fit so perfectly.

Closing his eyes, he leans into my touch, looking serene and satisfied. He looks so different; lighter, hopeful, and the realization that he's been unhappy for a while is like a punch to the gut.

Sliding my hand to the back of his neck, I lower his face to mine so our lips are a breath apart.

A glutton for punishment, I ask him one more time. "Are you sure about this?"

"Kiss me, Jordan," he demands, his voice steady and sure. "Kiss me, and let me show you just how sure I am."

9

———

GAEL

EVEN THOUGH MY words sound like I'm in control, the way Jordan moves us up the bed and fuses his mouth to mine tells me otherwise.

With both of us on our sides, our bodies facing one another, the kiss starts slowly. It's soft and unhurried. There's no rush, no frenzy. No fear or urgency, just a languid pace that makes this feel like more than a fleeting moment.

The simplicity makes it feel like we have forever to explore, like there isn't an expiration date and it isn't something either one of us can deny.

Pulling back, he stares at me, his blue eyes no longer the eye of a storm, but rather calm and full of awe. "I could do this forever."

"I want you to," I reply before locking my lips with his, not wanting to waste even a split second with words. I move my mouth against his, coaxing his tongue to meet mine, knowing this is the only form of communication either one of us needs right now.

His hand glides down my arm, resting comfortably on

my hip. Wanting to be closer, and loving the freedom to do so, I hook my leg over his side and press my erection against him.

Jordan groans at the contact, and I'm not surprised by the presence of his own hard-on. Now cupping my ass, he pushes our groins closer, needing friction and deepening the kiss.

I can feel the return of the frenzy, but now it isn't about time or take backs. It's not a rush against the real world. His kiss now is less reserved, less cautious. Jordan kisses me the way you kiss a partner. The way you kiss your lover.

The hunger and desperation ramp up, and our tongues are now dueling for dominance. He expertly rubs his covered shaft against mine, and I revel in all the new sensations. In all the things I wanted but could never have. His strength, his size. His touch, his taste.

Him.

Our kisses are effortless.

The feel of him is perfection.

In this moment, he's both the boy of my past and the man of my future, and finally, together, it feels right.

"Is this okay?" he murmurs against my lips. "I know you haven't done–"

Silencing him, I slide my own hand up and underneath his shirt, passing his taut abs and resting on his pec. "It's more than okay."

He groans as I purposefully use my thumb to circle his nipple, and my dick jerks in excitement at the prospect of learning this side of Jordan. What he likes, what turns him on, what drives him absolutely crazy.

I repeat the action, this time watching the way he bites on his bottom lip in restraint. "That bad, huh?" I tease.

Smirking, he shakes his head. "You're going to kill me, you know that? You touching me... fuck."

"Just be with me how you would anyone else."

"But you're not anyone else." In one swift moment, he pushes me onto my back and straddles me. "Don't you know that yet?"

Jordan lowers his mouth to the side of my neck, just below my ear. "You're the guy I've wanted like this for so very long." His lips skate down to my collarbone and back up. Over and over while his hands push my shirt up my torso until we're both tugging it off my body.

Like a magnet, his mouth is back on my skin, kissing and licking, memorizing the landscape of my chest and shoulders with his mouth.

Sitting up, Jordan looks down at my body, his eyes devouring me, his hips expertly rolling over mine. "You're my teenage wet dream." His voice is low and full of lust. "My adult fantasy."

"Tell me about them." My hands find purchase on his waist, guiding him to pick up the pace. "Tell me about the dreams and the fantasies, and everything in between."

"And if I scare you?"

"The only thing you're doing is getting me so fucking hard." And it was true. Harder than I'd ever been was an understatement for the way my body felt. Anticipation and adrenaline swim through my veins. My heart full, and my cock aching with a heavy need I don't ever remember feeling.

Chuckling, he bends down and captures my mouth in a chaste kiss before murmuring, "You're blowing my mind."

"I'd rather you blow me," I retort, without giving it a second thought. It's a casual joke that slips out of my mouth with the same ease as our lifelong friendship, and it unintentionally cuts through the last layer of hesitancy between us.

"You gonna let me put my mouth on you?" he asks with a smirk, the smart-ass lilt to his voice only making him sexier. "I'll suck you so fucking good."

Wanting it all, I take a fistful of his shirt in my hands, dragging him down to me and smashing his mouth to mine. His hands race down my stomach with purpose, gripping the waistband of my jeans and unbuckling my belt. Dexterous fingers undo the button of my jeans and then slide the zipper down.

"Lift your hips up," he orders as he scoots farther down my legs.

I raise them up, and he swiftly yanks both my jeans and my briefs down to my thighs, and my hard shaft springs free, slapping my stomach.

Resting on his haunches, his eyes drop to my cock, his body rising and falling with every breath he manages to take. I watch him drink me in, enjoying the way it feels to have his eyes on me. The way it feels to be wanted by him. Touched by him.

The way it feels to be with *him*.

"Remember that time we fought over the broken Play-Station controller and who was going to tell your parents about it?"

His gaze is now on mine while his hands roughly pull out his own dick. "Remember we wrestled until you tapped out?"

"I didn't tap out," I correct him.

"Remember when I got on top of you like this?"

"How could I forget?" I make a fist around my own cock. "You jumped off me so fucking fast."

He tucks his boxers underneath his balls and slides his

hand up and down, stroking himself. "Because this was all I could imagine." Our hands move in tandem as he continues. "You underneath me. Our cocks out."

I let the words of his filthy fantasy spur me on as I tighten the grip on myself, mesmerized by the way the foreskin of his uncut cock plays hide-and-seek with his slick head.

"What else would you have done?" I ask, my voice thick and hoarse.

"I would've watched until you made yourself come."

"That it?" I tease, my eyes stuck to the up and down motion of his hands. "I thought it would be more of a show."

"You've got no fucking idea." Reaching out, he tips my chin up so our eyes meet. "I'm not rushing a single fucking thing with you."

Leaning over me, he presses his lips to mine. I have every intention to get lost in the kiss while stroking myself, but when he swats my hand away and slides his cock against mine, my whole body shudders.

"I'm going to make you lose your fucking mind," he murmurs against my mouth. "I'm going to make it so you can't breathe without thinking about me."

"I already do that," I say, my breathing ragged, my focus all over the place. His hand wraps around the both of us, jerking us both, and I'm hypnotized by the way his hot, slick skin feels against mine. The friction. The slide. The promise of so much pleasure.

"I'm going to drive you as crazy as I feel," he threatens.

"Fuck. Jordan," I groan. "I'm going to come."

"Don't even think about it," he warns. "I need to put my mouth on you first."

He shimmies his body down my legs till his head is in direct line with my dick and his fingers grip around the base; the sight alone has my balls tightening. "Damn, you've got a beautiful fucking cock."

"Best you've ever seen?" I ask, sitting up on my elbows so I can get a better look at him between my legs.

His tongue slips between his lips and circles the head of my cock, teasing and taunting. "Best I've ever tasted too."

His eyes never leave mine, the blue so potent, the desire discernible as he spears the tip into the slit of my crown and tastes my pre-come.

"Please, Jordan," I beg, desperate for more.

"Please what?"

"Please," I repeat, knowing my ability to form a coherent sentence is severely compromised. I extend my hand and glide my fingers through his hair and grip. "Please."

Holding my gaze, his stare never falters, the connection between our eyes alone intensifying the hum pulsing through my body. With the simplest of looks, he consumes me, and when he covers my crown with his hot, wet mouth and sucks, it takes all my willpower not to blow my load that very second.

Jordan pops his mouth off, and his hand continues with the delicious torture, moving up and down my shaft. He changes his rhythm and licks the underside of my length and then sucks on my balls before alternating between relentlessly touching me and tasting me.

Unable to hold myself up any longer, I drop my elbows from their position and let my body sag onto the mattress. I keep my hands in his hair, needing to touch some part of him, as he expertly navigates his mouth, his tongue, and his hands around my leaking cock; finding all the ways to light my nerve endings on fire.

Jordan drags his lips up my dick and lets go of me with a

pop. "I want you to fuck my mouth," he orders. A jolt of electricity races through me at his request. "I don't want to ever forget how desperate I'm about to make you."

Full of nothing but that exact desperation he's referring to, I jerk my hips up in the direction of his mouth. "Less talking. More sucking," I rasp.

The salacious smirk that appears on his face promises nothing but torture, and God, how I want it. I want exactly what he promised and to lose myself under his touch.

His mouth returns to my cock, but this time there's no finesse. Every lick is driven by need, and every suck is greedy. His head bobs up and down my dick, every stroke deeper than the one before. And when I feel myself hit the back of his throat, my body arches off the bed.

"Fuck," I groan, thrusting my hips up toward his mouth. "I'm so close."

Jordan moves faster, getting deep enough his face presses up against my groin, and I wish we could stay this way forever. Drowning in each other.

Like a warning, heat spreads throughout my body, from the top of my head to the tips of my toes. Holding him in place, I fuck his face just like he asked, harder and more desperate than I've ever been before.

The sound of him gagging on my cock echoes around us, pushing me over the familiar edge.

When I feel a finger ghost over the crease of my ass, my imagination runs wild with possibilities, sending my body into a collection of spasms as my orgasm, and years of repressed feelings and sexual tension, roll through me.

"Oh, fuck." My chest heaves, rising up and down, every breath loud and long. I glance down at Jordan, who's now up on his knees, looking smug and satisfied, and I can't help but offer up a lazy smile.

His dick is still jutting out of his pants, all long and hard and straining. And when he makes a fist around himself, I can't help but sit up and reach for him.

Shaking his head, he swats my hand away. "I won't last."

My gaze flickers between his face and his cock. Loving the concentration in his expression and the lascivious way he's touching himself. "I don't care," I tell him. Because I don't. I just want to feel him in any way I can.

I wrap my hand around his and let him set the pace. I follow his lead until he loosens his hold on himself and allows me to take control.

Capturing my lips with his, Jordan kisses me senseless while I stroke him.

Just as he predicted, it only takes a few tugs and he's groaning through his release and warm, sticky streams of come decorate my hand.

Closing his eyes, he rests his forehead against mine. Even though he's breathing heavily, he manages a light chuckle. "That wasn't very impressive, was it?"

"I don't know what you're talking about, I just got the best blowjob of my life."

He opens his eyes to look at me. "The best, huh?"

The question doesn't hide both his insecurities and vulnerabilities, and I wonder how many times he's going to play the comparison game with himself.

Wanting to steer us both away from anything that even remotely touches on Elena, I bring my come covered hand to my mouth and begin to lick the evidence of his pleasure off my fingers.

I feel his eyes on me as I continuously suck on my digits.

"How's your first taste of my come?" he asks.

"I like anything that's yours," I quip.

He launches himself at me, and we both fall onto the mattress, our clothes still haphazardly on, our bodies covered in a sheen of sweat.

Laying atop me, he seals his mouth to mine, kissing me without a care in the world. Kissing me like we have all the time in the world.

I wrap my arms around him, loving the way he fits against me. Loving how touching him and having him touch me has deepened a connection I didn't think could get any stronger.

"You're a really good kisser," he says in between kisses.

Smiling against his mouth, I ask, "Not what you expected?"

Pulling back, he props himself up on his elbows. "Honestly, I didn't know what to expect. I didn't..." He doesn't finish the sentence, shaking his head instead. "Never mind."

"Hey, you can tell me anything." I squeeze him to me. "That offer has never been, nor will it ever be, conditional."

"Shower with me?"

It's not what I wanted him to say, but I don't press. We manage to get ourselves off the bed and, hand in hand, head to the bathroom. When we're naked and under the hot spray, he turns me away from him and starts massaging the body wash into my shoulders.

"I tried not to let myself imagine this often."

Knowing that Jordan's more than likely to elaborate on what's in his heart if we're not face-to-face, I stay silent and wait with bated breath for everything and nothing all at once.

In silence, his soapy hands roam around my body. They glide over my skin, down my arms, over my nipples, and down to my semi-hard cock.

I let my head fall back to his shoulder as he slowly strokes my shaft, plumping it back to full mast.

"But even when I did," he finally continues, pressing his own erection against my ass. "It was never like this."

Spinning me around, he pushes me till my back hits the hard, wet tiled wall. He adjusts our cocks, side by side, while his eyes never leave mine.

"I could never have prepared myself for this." He wraps his fingers around us both and glides his hand up and down.

Tilting my head down to his mouth, I catch his bottom lip between my own. "Prepared yourself for what?" I murmur. I continue to press kisses on his jaw and around the corner of his mouth while my dick throbs with arousal. "Tell me."

In an almost growl, he kisses me back, his lips hard on mine. "It's never going to be enough. How much I want you. It's never going to be enough."

He sounds like a mad man, but I just kiss him through it, knowing exactly how he feels. Giving ourselves permission to feel the way we do and to breathe life into our love instantly changed what we felt from a simmering boil to a complete emotional obliteration.

It's all-consuming, and that sated, calm-like feeling we felt after our orgasms seems distant and almost unattainable every time we touch.

Jordan's hand falls away from my dick, and the loss has me momentarily breaking the kiss.

"Watch me," he orders.

I follow his gaze to where he uses both hands to align the heads of our cocks. With expertise I don't even want to think about, he smoothly sheaths my crown with his foreskin.

"Oh, fuck," I breathe out.

Enveloped in a tight cocoon of warmth, I'm enraptured by the way he slides the skin over most of my dick, my slick head nudging his.

My mind seems unable to do anything but focus on the way we're connected. At how the eroticism of this one action confirms I've been trudging through life with rose-colored glasses. But now, I can see.

I see the filth, the fantasy, the future.

Feeling my knees weaken, I let the wall behind me hold my weight as Jordan's hands seduce me into my next orgasm.

"Feel this," he rasps out, grabbing one of my hands. Under his instruction, I wrap my fingers around myself, holding his foreskin in place, relishing in the way his cock completely swallows mine.

When he starts thrusting into my fist, a loud groan leaves my mouth, the glide of his dick atop mine so different to what we'd done before.

It's both intimate and carnal, the perfect slide of pre-come between us. How each stroke heightens the way the ridges and veins of his cock rub against mine.

Together, we find a perfect rhythm. And as the water spraying over us turns lukewarm, I'm sure my body is going to burn from the inside out.

"I'm going to come," Jordan pants. "Don't let go."

Agreeing wordlessly, my grip on us tightens as I buck my hips with purpose. Raising his free hand to the wall, Jordan's movements become frantic. Vigorous.

"Kiss me," I beg. "Fuck. Please."

He smashes his mouth to mine, and we're all teeth and tongues, gorging on one another like starved animals. My body convulses without warning, and I whimper into his mouth as my orgasm slams through me.

In less than a second, I feel his cock pulse underneath my fingers. He presses his lips to mine, hard and bruising, as thick, hot liquid floods the tunnel we've created, and his pleasure exquisitely melds with mine.

Lips parting, we both stare at each other before glancing down, our thoughts in sync.

I release my hold on us and follow the way Jordan drags himself off my shaft. He leaves a glistening trail of sticky come in his wake, and I love that there's no telling whether it's his or mine.

Softly, but firmly, I squeeze the softening tip of his cock, thrilled by the drops of come that slide between my fingers.

Raising my hand to his mouth, I offer him a taste, and he obliges.

"Fuck, that was hot," I tell him as he licks my skin. "We need to do that again."

Teasingly, he bites one of my fingers and winks at me. "I'll do it as many times as you want."

10

JORDAN

AFTER OUR SHOWER LAST NIGHT, we managed to finally make it to bed, where we ignored the constant beeps and vibrations of our cell phones and stayed up late exploring one another.

It didn't matter how right it all felt, I was still playing devil's advocate with myself.

I didn't have the stomach to bring up Elena and did my best not to think of her. I was a hypocrite, saying I wouldn't go any further, and now we were both too far gone.

The rest of the world faded into nothing as I touched and tasted him and drew an invisible line for myself while I was with him. Wanting to feel him but not wanting to overwhelm him. It didn't matter how confident he seemed, there were things I wouldn't do while there was still a chance he could regret it.

With every kiss and touch and taste, I rationalized it with a new limit, with a new concession, with some asinine justification that this was really going to work out for us.

I woke up in the middle of the night more than once

and just stared at him beside me, wondering how I was going to survive losing him.

I wanted the confidence he had, but instead, I settled for the memories I'd have to hold on to when he went back to her.

I would never forget this time together. The closeness. The truths. The pleasure.

Even if he walked away, I would always have this. We both would. These handful of hours that were ours, always. No matter what awaited us outside these closed doors.

Deciding to get started on the day, and thinking we probably should make up for bailing on everyone last night, I lean over and press a soft kiss to his forehead before heading to the bathroom.

Smiling like a loon, I step into the shower, remembering what we did together and how good it felt. I try not to get too lost in thought, but my thickening cock has other plans.

Knowing Gael will need the shower, and that we don't really have time—as tempting as it would be—to fuck around, I ignore my erection and clean up as quickly as possible.

When I exit the bathroom, he's sitting up, the bedding covering him from the waist down. His hair is all tousled, reminding me of just how many times I ran my fingers through it.

He's on the phone, and when he notices my presence, he straightens his back, holding my stare, and I know with absolute certainty it's Elena on the other end. "Yeah. Jordan just finished getting ready," he tells her. "I'll talk to you later on."

His eyes never leave mine as he finishes up the conversation, and I try my hardest not to let reality slip in and snuff out my high.

He doesn't linger on the phone call, eventually dragging the cell from its place between his ear and shoulder and dropping it onto the mattress.

The phone call and Elena evaporate into thin air as he tilts his head to the side and lets his eyes roam my body. His gaze stops at the towel around my waist, and any hesitation I expected has vanished and I'm suddenly wishing I jerked off in the shower after all.

"I'm never going to get used to you looking at me that way," I confess.

He chuckles. "I'm never going to get used to not having to hide it."

Moving toward him, I stand at the edge of the bed instead of sitting beside him. I wordlessly look down at the phone and then back at him, the question loud in my silence.

A loud exhale leaves his mouth as he reaches for my hand and tugs at it, urging me to sit down. I do as he wants, but I keep a safe distance, as if I can still protect myself after last night.

"I don't know what I'm supposed to do here," he says. "Elena and I can keep pushing our circle-shaped relationship into a square-shaped hole till the end of time, but it's time to admit it's never going to fit." Unshed tears fill his honest and vulnerable eyes, the toll this is taking on him no longer hidden by his bravado. "But I don't want to break anyone's heart."

He tries to look away, but my hands keep him in place. I want the truth and I want to be there for him, manage my insecurities and support him at the same time, even if those two things don't align. "Don't hide how you feel. Talk to me."

I watch his throat move as he tries to compose himself.

"I feel guilty," he admits. "But then you're here, touching me and kissing me, and that feeling just..." He shrugs. "I can't find that guilt when I'm with you, and I don't know what kind of person that makes me."

Scooting up the bed and closer to him, I grab his face between my hands. "You mean what kind of people that makes us? I hate putting you in this position. I hate knowing you have to break her heart." I run my thumb across his lips. "Tell me what you need; tell me how I can make this easier."

He mirrors my actions and places his palms on my cheeks. "Just... please don't get cold feet on me."

Considering the circumstances, I feel like I should be asking this of him, but I know why he's scared. I know my fears are responsible for the last ten years. For the hurt I caused us both.

"Promise me," he insists. "Because I want this, and it might not be easy, but I want this life with you."

Nodding, I push away the fear and anxiety and press my lips to his forehead. "I promise."

"So, we'll just keep it to ourselves, until you talk to Elena," I suggest, wanting to somehow make it easier for him. "Whenever that is."

"Are you sure?"

"You think I don't know how hard this is going to be?" I lower my mouth to his and declare my commitment with kisses I can no longer hold back. "How hard it's going to be to explain this to everyone?" Kiss. "I'm not going to abandon you in your hardest moment." Kiss. "Especially not when we're both responsible." Kiss. "Together doesn't just mean when the going's good."

This time he kisses me, his lips lingering on mine, a

simple—yet worth a thousand words—connection. "Thank you."

I wink at him and move back, putting some space between us. "I think we're going to need to make up for abandoning everyone last night."

"I want to feel bad, but..."

"Then don't," I finish, smiling at him. "I wouldn't trade last night for anything. So, until we can do it again, how about we meet up with the guys for breakfast and plan the rest of the day."

"When did you say the car thing was?"

"Tomorrow," I supply. "I figured it was the perfect way to kick off the new year."

He looks at me pensively. "What is it?"

"I feel bad you spent all this money on my 'bachelor party.'" He hooks his fingers, motioning air quotes.

"Don't feel bad, because I don't think last night would've happened if I didn't spend all this money on your 'bachelor party.'" I mimic his air quotes. "Plus, it isn't like we've never wanted to come to Vegas together and do this shit."

Unexpectedly, there's a knock at our door and Seth's voice booms through the room. "You guys up yet?"

Feeling like we just got caught, I stand up off the bed in a rush. "Yeah, Gael is just in the shower," I lie. "We'll be out in a bit."

"Okay. But don't take too long, we're fucking hungover and starving."

"Got it," I shout back.

When I make a move toward the wardrobe, I feel myself being pulled back by my towel. I look over my shoulder at Gael. "What are you doing?"

He gives me a wicked smirk, and I just know the next words out of his mouth are going to lead to trouble.

"I'm going to have to keep my hands off you all fucking day," he informs me, as if I don't know. "So let me look at you for a little while longer."

He tugs my towel to the ground, and I can't help but turn to face him. To give him the view he was desperately seeking.

I craved to have him stare at me this way; I'd wanted it for so long. For him to be practically drooling over me, to be infatuated with my appearance.

It was fucking superficial, but it meant something to me.

When he licks his lips, I grab my now stiff cock, forgetting all about where we need to be and who's waiting for us. "Fuck. I want to feed you my cock when you lick your lips like that."

"Anyone ever tell you your mouth is fucking filthy?" he says with a smile.

"You got a problem with it?"

He drags the white sheet off his own body, revealing his hard cock and heavy balls. "Not at all."

I leap toward him, unable to keep my hands to myself.

Dragging him to the edge of the bed, I stand between his parted legs and waste no time getting on my knees. "I need you to fuck my mouth."

He wraps his hand around his shaft and starts to jerk it. "I didn't hear you say please," he teases.

"There's no fucking time for please." My fingers make a fist around the base of his shaft, and I waste no time covering his crown with my mouth.

He moans, sliding his hands through my hair, gripping the strands with much more urgency than last night.

Wanting to get him there quickly, I pull out all the stops. My sole intention to drive him wild, and fast.

I suck and lick. I suck and lick. I suck and lick.

Wanting nothing more than to feel him explode, I lap up the salty preview of what's to come. I slide my mouth off with a pop and then glide my tongue up and down the underside of his cock. I revel in the way his skin feels against my tongue, the way my taste buds not only taste him, but feel him.

They feel the lines of his masculinity. They feel the length of his lust. They feel the steady pulse of his longing.

I bring my mouth to his balls and suck on each one.

"Fuuuck," he groans, tugging at my hair. "Do it again."

I repeat the motion and then lift his sac and tease his taint. His loud moans fill the room, and it takes all my strength to not explore his hole with my tongue.

"That's next," I threaten, my own erection impossibly hard. "Now put a pillow over your face so they don't hear you."

I return my attention back to his dick, loving the way he writhes underneath me as I sheath him with my mouth.

I lick and suck. Lick and suck. Lick and suck.

My eyes water, and I gag repeatedly as his hips greedily thrust upward. His thick cock stretches my lips, hitting the back of my throat. And we're nothing but give and take as he fucks my mouth, racing to reach his release.

"Fuck. That's it," he pants. "That's it. That's it. That's it."

A rush of come spills into my mouth just as I look up to see Gael smothering his face with a pillow. His body quivers and quakes as I take my time swallowing every single drop.

Letting him fall from my mouth, I rise up on my feet as

he falls back on the bed in a sated heap. Climbing over him, I lower my mouth to his, forcing him to taste himself.

"Are you ever going to let me taste you?" he asks nervously.

My already throbbing cock leaks at the thought, but I don't let my hormones answer his question.

"If you're comfortable." I drop another kiss on his lips. "But I'd be happy to love up on you forever with nothing in return. Letting me touch you. Watching you unravel like this. For me, it's the greatest fucking gift I could ever receive."

"I want to watch you unravel for me."

"Tonight," I promise. "Tonight, I'm at your mercy."

He glances down at my erection. "You're still hard."

"We don't have time for me." It would take the simplest of touches for me to blow my load, but I want to show him it isn't always just about getting off for me. It's an added bonus.

But watching *him* in the throes of ecstasy? I live for that. The freedom to touch him, to please him. The privilege to love him.

"Every time you look at me today, imagine me just like this." I straighten my body and grip my cock. "Hard and dripping, waiting to fuck your virgin mouth."

He swallows hard, his eyes pools of desire. "Promise me your mouth will be just as filthy then as it is now."

"I promise it'll be filthier."

———

"I'M SO FUCKING FULL." Seth groans, rubbing his stomach. "I need a nap."

"A nap?" Gael scoffs. "You spent ten minutes telling

Jordan and me off for being late, and now you want to go back to bed? Not happening."

Ray slaps Seth on the back. "I guess the groom has spoken."

I feel my face scrunch up at hearing Gael referred to as the groom. It takes me a few seconds too long to rid myself of the expression, and when I look around the table to see if anyone noticed, I catch Julian staring at me with a little too much curiosity in his eyes.

Feeling as if he can see right through me, I look away. Not because I feel guilty, but because I don't want to be the reason any of this comes out before Gael is ready for it to.

Even though I'm probably not noticeably sitting closer to Gael than usual, my want, my desire to wrap him up in my arms and kiss him whenever I want, has me moving my body away from his.

Julian raises an eyebrow at me, and I want to kick myself for single-handedly making this breakfast more awkward than it needs to be.

Trying to play it cool, I slide myself off the rest of the bench-style seat and rise to my feet. "I'm going to quickly head to the bathroom," I tell them. Gael glances up at me, and I know he's using all his willpower to not follow me.

The hint of even a single moment alone is like the temptation of alcohol to an addict, and I know one of us has to be the cautious one.

I would assume years of hiding how I've felt about him would have prepared me for this, but then I remember what he said back in the room last night. *"Sometimes, I'd catch you looking at me. And that look... I knew that look. I knew it, because I felt it"* And I acknowledge it will be a fucking miracle if either of us manages to get through this trip without anybody catching on to the change between us.

If I thought it was near impossible to forget about the kiss we shared ten years ago, I know for certain last night's activities will be forever burned in my memory. Knowing what we did, and knowing that while we're here we can do it again and again and again, has me giddy.

I don't waste time turning away from the table, and away from Gael's desperate eyes, and Julian's knowing stare.

I may be determined to keep the secret, but the universe has no plans on making it easy. On either of us.

When I'm finished in the bathroom, I return to the table and find Ray slipping money into the leather folder before handing it to the server.

Dragging my wallet out of my back pocket, I pluck out a few bills and put them in the center of the table.

"No way," Ray scolds. "You've paid plenty. Breakfast was on me." He picks up the cash and literally throws the bills at me. "Plus, what would my wife think if I didn't take care of her brother? It's bad enough I have to hear how amazing you are all the time," he adds with a playful smirk. "Thank God you're gay, because I'm almost certain she would've married you instead of me."

The table erupts in laughter at his comment, and I find the levity I needed to get out of my own head until Gael says, "It wouldn't have mattered. Even before he came out, I told them he was off-limits."

"What? Why?" Seth interjects. "Wanted to keep him for yourself?"

It's supposed to be a joke. A variation of something he and everybody else has said to us a million times. But this time, the thought that maybe, even back then, he was staking his claim, makes my heart expand inside my chest.

A ridiculous flutter builds in my stomach, accompanied by a smile that is far too private for such a public place.

Gael catches it, and I watch him as he bites the inside of his cheek and turns back to face everyone else at the table.

I lower my gaze to the floor and shove my hands in my pockets, unable to wipe the smile off my face and needing to hide it.

But when I hear Julian call out to Gael from across the table, I know I wasn't quick enough.

11

———

GAEL

"GAEL," Julian calls out.

I glance over at him expectantly. "Yeah?"

"Do you guys mind if I borrow Gael for a bit?" he asks the table. Deacon turns to look at him, wondering what he's talking about, but a quick squeeze of the shoulder assures him that Julian will explain it later.

I scan all their faces, thinking this is some surprise they've planned, but when I catch sight of Jordan's face, I glance back at Julian and know immediately why he wants to talk.

"Everything okay?" I ask.

"Yeah. I just wanted to show you something."

I've known him long enough to know he's lying, but since my gut tells me I'm sure I would rather have this conversation in private, I follow him out of the diner and into the open-spaced walkway.

When I avoid his gaze, I hear him huff in annoyance. "So, you're going to make me drag it out of you?"

I shrug nonchalantly. "I don't know what you're talking about."

"You're so lucky your brothers-in-law are fucking clueless, because you are a terrible liar."

"What am I lying about?"

"What happened last night?"

"I sent you a text telling you I was tired so I went to bed. Didn't you get it?"

"Really?" He tilts his head at me pointedly. "That's how you want to do this?"

Looking back into the diner, I see Jordan sitting back down at the table and trying to subtly look my way. Exhaling loudly, my eyes return to Julian. "It's not how I want to do this," I tell him. "It's just that I still need to do a few things first."

"You're calling off the wedding, aren't you?" I press my lips together, because I so desperately want to tell him. He tries another angle, persisting with all different types of questions. "All this time I've given you shit about how he feels, and you never once said you felt anything back. So you two are going to act platonic all weekend?" When I turn my head to look away from him, he swats me in the middle of my chest. "Did you sleep with him?"

"No," I retort. "We didn't get that far."

I groan in frustration when I realize what I've said. Dragging my hands down my face in resignation, I let out a loud sigh before facing Julian.

"I love him," I say with a soft shrug. "I've always loved him."

"Gael," he scolds. "Why didn't you tell me?"

"What difference would it have made?"

"I could've saved you from this mess if you'd confided in me." He looks a little crestfallen. "I never would have judged you. It's not like I don't know how hard it is to want something you don't think you should have."

I think of him and Deacon and how happy they are and their struggle to get to where they are today.

"I know he's worth it."

Julian gives his head a quick shake. "I'm not saying he isn't. And quite frankly, it's your business." He extends his hand and squeezes my shoulder. "I just don't want you to feel like you have to hide it from me."

"I just… can we walk and talk?" I ask him.

Wordlessly, he begins to walk away from the storefront, and I fall into step beside him. "I just don't want Ray and Seth finding out before we all get back to Seattle. I don't need them running their mouths to my sisters."

"I can understand that," he supplies with a nod. "And Elena?"

I think back to the conversation Jordan and I had this morning, and everything that's transpired between us since last night. And I've never felt such equal amounts of relief and dread, about all of it.

The man I've always wanted was finally within my reach, and there was no way around the collateral damage that my choices were going to cause.

Deep in my gut, I know Elena would recover, but that didn't mean she wouldn't hurt, nor would she forgive me. And when I allowed myself to leave the bubble Jordan and I had created over the last twenty-four hours, remorse over our lost future sat like a heavy boulder in the pit of my stomach.

"I'm going to talk to her as soon as we get back," I tell him. "The quicker the better, because this weekend feels like a dream. But sneaking around and what not?" I shake my head. "I'm not doing that to her."

Grabbing my elbow, Julian stops me, forcing me to turn around and face him. "I know this isn't easy, and I wish it didn't have to come to this. For any of you. But real love, the right love, it's too hard to walk away from. And even though this isn't ideal, choosing that type of love doesn't make you a bad person."

Even though I know there's a lot of truth to what he's saying, I can't help the way it feels so much better to hear someone else say it.

"Thanks, man. I'm lucky to have you as a friend."

He just shrugs and smiles. "You're not too bad yourself."

On our way back to the diner, my phone vibrates in my pocket. I pull it out to see a text from Jordan.

Jordan: Are you okay? We've left the diner. Deacon and I are following Seth and Ray.

Me: What are they doing?

Jordan: They want to shop for a bit. Heading to the Forum at Caesars. If I know your sisters, they told them not to come home empty handed.

I laugh because it's exactly something my sisters would've said.

Me: Okay. We're coming back now. Won't be too far behind.

Jordan: Are you going to tell me what Julian wanted? I think I made it too obvious this morning. I'm sorry.

Me: It's not like he hasn't always known you've been in love with me. Some things are hard to hide.

I add the wink emoji, wanting our exchange to be light, wanting to rid him of any worry. This weekend, I just want us to *be*.

Jordan: *eye roll emoji* Get over yourself.

Chuckling, I tell him Julian and I will see him soon and then slide my cell back into my pocket.

When I look back at Julian, he too is busy on his phone. "Deacon?" I ask.

He nods and says, "Caesars?"

———

WHEN JULIAN and I meet up with the rest of the group, Jordan and Julian exchange a glance that puts Jordan at ease almost instantly. I wonder if the approval of others matters to him, or whether it's just specific to my friend.

Either way, the mood has shifted and the worry that anybody was paying any attention to Jordan and me is long gone. If anything, we're both a little reckless. We let our bodies brush and our hands touch while my heart thumps wildly in my chest.

I don't know what I love more, actually being with him, or the anticipation. Every part of me feels like it's alight for him, and I can see he feels the exact same way.

His cheeks are flushed, and his eyes rimmed with want and desire; it makes the hours we spend with everyone else feel like never-ending days.

When everyone is too busy looking around for things to buy, he comes up behind me, presses his hard cock against my ass, lowers his mouth to my ear, and whispers, "I told you I'd be hard all day for you."

I bite back a moan and shamelessly adjust my own erection, knowing he won't misunderstand the movement.

Before either of us can get too carried away, Seth and Ray return with Deacon and Julian, hand in hand, not far behind. I inwardly beg the universe that they're done with the search for their perfect presents and Jordan and I can go upstairs so I can literally throw myself at him.

"I think that's it," Ray announces. He turns to look at Julian and Deacon. "What about you guys?"

"Yeah, we're good," Julian supplies. He holds up a bag with what looks like two boxes of shoes. "We didn't really need any of this stuff anyway."

"Are you guys all keen to head back?" Jordan asks. "I think I need a nap."

"Same," I blurt out, just needing to be alone with him.

"Yeah, I think we could do with one too," Julian says, his eyes looking straight at me, his lips lifting in a smile.

I mouth the words "thank you," and try to shuffle us all out of the store and in the direction of the closest exit.

When we arrive at Aria, Seth surprises us when he asks, "Do you guys want to go swimming?"

"What?" Jordan asks, confused. "It's winter, aren't the pools closed?"

"Aria has a heated one," Seth responds. "And I can't tell you the last time I sat in a pool that served alcohol and was child free."

"You better be careful, man," I interject. "I'm starting to think you hate being shacked up with my sister."

He flips me the bird. "Just wait till you have kids."

Instead of that recent stab of loss I usually feel at the mention of children, I glance over to Jordan, imagining a life that seemed almost impossible for so long.

Just like earlier, when I mentioned telling my sisters he was off-limits, he smiles at me with so much love and devotion, and the need to be alone with him ratchets from high to an absolute necessity.

"I know you guys are tired, so it's cool if you don't want to," Seth adds.

He doesn't seem put out that we don't want to do the same things, but a sliver of guilt rushes through me as I think of the effort everyone made to spend the weekend together. To spend it with me.

I look over at Jordan, and, without exchanging a single word, he nods in understanding.

"I guess it can't be that much colder than home," I say with a shrug. "I don't know if I have anything to swim in, though, so that might be a bit of a problem."

When we reach the hotel, the six of us visit the souvenir store like the out-of-towners we were.

"We've only got these left," the sales clerk advises, pointing to a full rack of black swimming shorts with pink flamingos all over them. She eyes Jordan, her gaze roaming up and down the length of his body appreciatively. "Are you going swimming too?"

"We all are," I answer for him, irritated at the freedom she has to stare at him. "Do you have one in all of our sizes?" I snap.

Amused, Jordan gives me a wicked smirk before subtly glancing down to his crotch. Letting me know he finds my moment of insanity very appealing.

The outline of his dick is obvious through his jeans, but I do my best to pretend not to notice. Not to be affected. But it's useless.

Frustrated in more ways than one, I storm off to where the shorts are and pull off six that I think will fit each of us. When I reach the counter, I rush through paying and scoop the shorts up and walk to the guys.

Ray's brows knit together as he tries to keep up with my sudden mood change.

"Are you okay?" he asks while reaching for the shorts, looking through the sizes searching for a pair that'll fit him.

"I'm fine," I huff, feeling myself getting irrationally irritated by the second. Instead of waiting for them to figure out which pair belongs to whom, I meet Julian's eyes and hand him the pile of clothes.

Walking straight past Jordan, I beeline for the elevators, desperate to be behind closed doors. I don't wait, nor do I expect him to follow, but when a familiar hand stops the elevator door from closing, relief swallows me whole.

With my chest still rising and falling, I lean on the marble wall, needing the support, watching the door close behind him.

His eyes do a quick scan of the area, appreciating we're alone, before returning to mine. The air between us is charged and almost suffocating as he steps toward me with only one purpose.

His touch is rough and aggressive. Needy. He cups the back of my neck and greedily brings my mouth to his. Fisting his t-shirt, I drag him closer, pulling him flush against me, so tired of how hard we've had to work to keep our hands off each other.

The kiss is hard and desperate as we press pause on the rest of the world and play catch up. My mouth melds to his, apologizing for the lost moments. For the kiss I wanted to give him at breakfast. For the way his hand reached for mine every time we walked somewhere. For the way I wanted to look at him in public. To belong to one another for everyone to see.

The jolt of the elevator has us breaking the kiss, our breaths heavy. I hold on to his hand, not wanting to break the physical contact while a group of friends steps into the car, not giving us a second glance. And I love it. I love that we blend in, that we're not even worth a moment of their time.

I give Jordan's hand a squeeze, and he surprises me by leaning over and kissing my temple.

I smile, and I can feel it split my face in two.

This.

Moments like this are exactly why this is all worth it. The years of heartache. The years of separation. I would do it all again, knowing that, in the end, we get to have a lifetime of moments like this.

I turn my face to meet his, and Jordan drops soft kisses on my face. My eyes, the tip of my nose, my cheeks, then my lips.

The elevator stops again and the same group exits, leaving us alone.

Neither one of us moves, basking in the small moment of intimacy. I watch the floor numbers light up as we get higher and higher, closer to our suite.

"It feels like punishment watching you and not touching you," I say honestly. "I don't know how I did it all these years. And today"—I look back at him, shaking my head—"not touching you. I feel like I can't breathe."

Jordan pulls me into his arms, and we stand there in this empty elevator, hugging. Standing a little bit taller than me, he kisses the top of my head. "I would walk through fire to get to this side with you."

My chest squeezes as unshed tears fill my eyes at his declaration. I tighten my hold on him, pressing my lips to the hollow of his throat. "I was almost certain we were going to ravage each other, but I'm really enjoying the way you're holding me."

"Don't worry, I have no plans to let you go."

We finally make it to our floor, and in silence, we walk hand in hand through the suite and into our bedroom. We feel solid. Like the ground has shifted and now we're steady and the path ahead no longer feels unknown or undecided.

"Do we still need to go swimming?" I ask when he closes the bedroom door.

Much to my surprise, Jordan raises a hand that's holding two pairs of shorts.

"How did I not see you holding those?" I query.

"Eh." He shrugs. "I imagine it's hard for you to notice anything else when I walk into a room."

"Shut up." Even though he's a hundred percent right, I roll my eyes at him and snatch the shorts off him and toss them onto the bed. "Want to help me get undressed?"

I grip the edges of my shirt and begin to drag it up my body, when Jordan is right in front of me.

"Let me," he says hoarsely. "We don't have nearly enough time to do all the things I want to do to you, so let me just enjoy this."

Loving the way he takes control, I drop my hands and stand there, eager to feel him touch me. When my shirt comes off, I'm surprised to see him bringing the material up to his face. "I've always loved the way you smell," he confesses. "When we were younger, if your mom mixed up our laundry, I pretended not to notice just so I could have something of yours for that little bit longer."

He buries his face in it one more time before tossing it to the floor and lowering his mouth to my bare shoulder. "You always smelled like honey and home," he explains. "Sweet and familiar."

His lips skate across the top of my shoulder while his hands begin to unbutton my jeans. "I have a favor to ask you," he says, just as his hands dip beneath my waistband and wrap around my stiff cock.

"Anything," I breathe out.

"I know I don't have any right to make many demands, but I really want to ring in the new year with your mouth on mine." His hand begins to glide up and down my dick. "This next year is ours, Gael, and I don't want to play with fire and give the universe any other options."

Jordan has always been superstitious, and growing up with my mom, who lives and swears by rituals and traditions, only made it worse, so I'm not surprised by the request. No matter how many times I say this is it for me or this is us now, I'm slowly realizing his fear and insecurities will always be a voice in the background. He will always feel like something is ready to snatch it away unless he protects it in all the ways he knows how.

"We'll make our list of regrets and resolutions like we always do and then we'll end the night with your mouth on mine."

His hand moves faster now as my breathing gets heavier. My body aching for release.

"Promise me, Gael," he insists, his strokes now relentlessly determined to bring me to release. "Promise me you'll make it happen."

The demand and desperation in his voice escalates my arousal, my balls heavy, my skin burning.

"Promise. Me," he says through gritted teeth.

Pleasure licks up my spine as the first stream of come hits his hand. My body jolts as the orgasm rolls through me.

My voice is nothing but a breathless whisper, but I say what he so desperately needs to hear. "I promise."

12

JORDAN

NEW YEAR'S Eve in Vegas is bedlam. It's noisy and chaotic, but in the best type of way. The excitement and anticipation for whatever is on the horizon fuels people in a way that is infectious.

I've always loved New Year's. The idea of reflecting on the past and planning the future has grounded me for more years than I can count.

Growing up, it encouraged me to do better, to want more. And now, as an adult, I'm finally able to see what I've achieved. To acknowledge I'm no longer the boy who had nothing—nothing to lose and nobody to love.

But not this year.

After swimming, Gael indulged my need for tradition and we sat on the bed together, writing up our regrets and resolutions.

If anyone had told me at the beginning of this year we'd be here together, writing up resolutions for the both of us, with goals and plans for us to have and do together, I would've told them they'd lost their fucking mind.

This wasn't supposed to be my life, but I wasn't

complaining, nor was I ever going to let him go. I wasn't lying when I said I would walk through fire just to be here right now with him, like this.

The six of us had just finished dinner at a Brazilian BBQ restaurant that had come highly recommended by some guys I knew through work. I had booked it at the same time I booked the trip, because I knew none of us wanted to be walking around aimlessly and drunk like a bunch of twenty-one-year-olds in Vegas on New Year's.

The alcohol was flowing and the food was some of the best I had ever tasted. Seth and Ray were still obsessed with taking photos of everything in sight and I couldn't remember the last time I ever felt this relaxed.

"Now that you're in a better mood than you were at the gift shop, what's next on the agenda?" Ray asks before taking a sip of beer.

The smallest blush creeps up Gael's face, and I know he's embarrassed by how jealous he was, but instead of reacting to Ray's comments, he only addresses the question. "Don't act like you actually have plans to spend the rest of the night with us."

"What's that supposed to mean?" Seth interjects.

"Everybody here knows all you guys want to do is get back to the tables."

Ray gapes at us, pretending to be offended. "You make us sound like we're addicts."

"If the shoe fits," I add. "Just make sure you go back home with something more than an empty wallet."

"The only reason I have an empty wallet is because of the gifts I bought Mariana and the kids," Seth justifies.

"Are you guys willing to come with us to Fire?" Gael asks.

"The gay club?"

Fire is a franchise of gay clubs, and there's one in all major states across the US, and the one in Vegas is supposed to be one of the best.

"Um, how the hell are you going to get us into Fire on New Year's Eve?" Deacon interrupts.

"Have you even been to a gay club before?" I ask, wondering when he had time to plan this and why.

"It was my idea," Julian says. He's staring at Gael, a conspiratorial smile spread across his face. "I didn't want to come here without seeing what all the fuss was about, and Gael said he could pull some strings."

I swallow the lie because it's obvious they have a plan, and, honestly, I don't care where we are or what we're doing as long as we're together at midnight.

The group's focus returns to Seth and Ray. "Are you two coming?" Gael asks again.

They look at each other and have a silent conversation that has me chuckling to myself, because for all the shit they give Gael and me, they're just as close.

"We'll come for a bit," Seth says. "But don't be mad if we leave."

"You mean you're not going to stay and kiss me at midnight," I tease.

"I know you've been wanting on these lips for a couple of years now, but I'm sorry to say tonight's just not the night for it." He tips his chin toward Gael. "You've got Gael with you anyway. We all know he's the guy you really want." He winks, his usual jokes really hitting home. "You know the old saying, what happens in Vegas, stays in Vegas."

I steel my facial expressions as best I can, biting the inside of my cheek hard enough to bleed while Gael's fingers dig painfully into my thigh.

If only he knew.

———

THE MUSIC IS THUMPING in Fire, the atmosphere congruent with the way I'm feeling; alive and pulsating. The only one of our group left sitting in this horse-shaped booth Gael managed to score, I feel like a fucking king.

Every part of me is satiated. My mind, my body, my soul. I feel the more at ease and content than I ever have before. And there's no doubt it's all because of him.

Gael is on the dance floor, without a care in the world, getting lost in the rhythm, his body moving to the beat of the music, the strobe lights lighting him up like a beacon that calls to only me. He's always loved to dance, and I've always loved to watch.

But this time when I watch, there's no secret ogling, no hidden glances. I watch because I can. I watch because he's mine, and I watch enough for everyone else to know it too.

With only half an hour left till midnight, Seth and Ray are already long gone back to the casino to gamble, and Julian and Deacon are lost in the crowd. And if I were questioning why Gael had made plans to come to Fire, the freedom we're both feeling right now is all the answer I need.

Even through the sea of people and flashing lights, I feel Gael's gaze land on me. As if he's gliding on the dance floor, he makes his way through the bodies till he's standing between my widespread legs, holding his hands out for me to dance with him.

Wordlessly, I rise to my feet. I take hold of his hips and pull him close to me, ensuring he can feel how hard watching him dance gets me. "You're so fucking sexy," I growl into his ear.

He pulls me onto the dance floor, the crowd splitting for

us as we make our way to the middle. He wraps his hands around my neck and slips his leg in between mine. We sway and his erection repeatedly grazes over mine.

The friction is torture, a tease of the most delicious kind that I feel almost privileged to be able to experience right now.

My hands roam over his body, clutching his ass and pressing him into me, slipping underneath his shirt and basking in the heat emanating from his skin. I dip my head between his neck and shoulder, ghosting my lips over his pulse, loving the way it trips underneath my touch.

I lick and suck and bite at his skin as we gyrate against one another. Dancing like we're fucking, every part of me wishing we were, but knowing it's the one line I won't let him cross. No matter how badly I want it.

As if his thoughts are exactly in line with mine, Gael grabs my face, tilts his head and crushes his mouth to mine. His tongue sweeps over mine, over and over again, and I can taste the words I've felt for him, down to the marrow of my bones, for as long as I can remember.

I love you.

A loud voice booms through the club, forcing us apart. But when the DJ announces that the countdown is soon, I feel like I'm on the edge of a cliff, desperately awaiting the freefall.

Just as another announcement comes through signaling the twenty-second countdown, Julian and Deacon appear out of thin air. They don't even blink twice at our embrace, and my heart expands at the simple show of acceptance and support.

Maybe this will be okay.

At ten seconds left, the crowd begins to chant every number in unison. But I don't take my eyes off Gael.

I stare at him in silence, and because the wall between us has finally been torn down, like a movie reel, I see everything I spent ten years trying to deny.

His love for me.

The way it grew.

The way it changed.

The way it could be.

The way it *will* be.

The whole club erupts in screams and cheers as the clock strikes midnight, and I wipe the single lone tear that unexpectedly decides to slide down my face.

"I love you," I mouth. The enormity of finally being able to say those words directly to him without fear or rejection, has me basking in complete euphoria. My knees feel weak, and my heart feels like it could fly right out of my chest.

"I love you."

Against the backdrop of the New Year's celebrations, we declare our love in three silent words that hold the key to very loud promises. Gael collapses into my arms, squeezes me tight, and brings his mouth to my ear. "Let's get out of here."

Needing him alone just as much, we wish Deacon and Julian a happy new year, and make plans on when and where to meet tomorrow.

As I shake Julian's hand goodbye, he pulls me into a hug and shouts above the music, "Take care of each other."

Pulling apart, I nod in acknowledgment and agreement. Gael is mine, and I always take care of what's mine.

Desperate and giddy, we brave the crowds and eventually make it to the suite. I'm grateful there's nobody else inside, even though I don't think it would've stopped either one of us. I drag him into the bedroom and walk him to the edge of the bed.

I want to ravage him. I want to make him groan and moan and writhe in desperation under my touch. I want to dive headfirst into every temptation and desire, but I restrain myself from reaching out to touch him and let Gael take the lead.

"What do you want?" he asks me.

A slight, incredulous chuckle leaves my mouth. "I don't think either of us are ready for that answer."

He grips my head in his hands and presses a soft kiss against my lips. There's no reassuring or dissuading between us, he just takes the lead and I wait, at his mercy.

His hands begin to unbutton my shirt. Neither fast or slow, only precise and purposeful.

When he pulls my shirt over my head, tosses it on the floor, and reaches for my jeans, impatience consumes me. Mirroring his actions, I try to catch up, wanting to touch him, and wanting to feel his skin.

Once every stitch of clothing is piled on the floor, we fall onto the bed in a tangled heap.

"Happy New Year," Gael murmurs against my mouth.

I wordlessly return the sentiment by smashing my mouth to his in a hungry kiss and beginning to rut against him. Entranced by the feel of his skin and the taste of his mouth, neither one of us comes up for air, physical touch the only sustenance either one of us wants and needs.

Gael wraps a leg around my waist, bringing my body flush with his, and my fingers curl themselves around his hair. Our kisses deepen, and the ache for more intensifies.

My hands and mouth can't get enough of him, kissing and sucking at his neck, tweaking and rolling his nipples. Using everything I have in my repertoire, I lick down his sternum and then trace the dips and valleys of his abdomen. I brush my lips over the smattering of hair that lines his stomach, my cock impossibly hard at all my favorite little reminders that I'm with a man.

When I came out as gay, I remember finally feeling so certain in myself and who I was. I couldn't hold the lie in anymore, and saying those words aloud gave me freedom from my own mental prison. And with every passing touch, a hug or a kiss, every milestone of shared physical contact solidified that my attraction to men was very much a part of my identity.

But only right now, as I slide my mouth onto Gael's cock, teasing him. As I drag my tongue down his length and suck on his balls. As the room fills with nothing but Gael's breathy moans, and my hands raise his legs and push his thighs open. As my tongue follows his taint and dips, for the very first time, inside his hole, I feel like it was all worth it.

The hard parts. The sleepless nights. The fears and the fights. The rejection.

The years without him. The years of wanting him. Of longing for him.

Every single shitty thing I both felt and was made to feel about being who I am has all been worth it, as if the universe was leading me to this.

His body jolts off the bed at the foreign intrusion, and an inferno of heat races through my veins, knowing this is a first for him.

I raise my eyes to meet his. "Tell me how it feels. I want to hear in detail how I'm driving you fucking crazy."

"I didn't know," he says with a shudder. "I didn't know that I'd want that."

"Keep talking," I demand, lowering my mouth back to the most intimate part of him.

"Oh, fuck," he pants, gliding his hands into my hair and pushing my face closer to him. "I feel so... oh, fuck."

"You feel?"

"Fuck," he groans. "Fuck. Fuck. Fuck."

My own cock throbs as my mouth and tongue make it their mission to drive Gael out of his mind. Bringing him to new heights, showing him new things.

Loving the sound of his voice and the chants of anguished pleasure that echo around the room, I bring a finger to my mouth and suck on it before pushing it inside him.

He's warm and tight, and I can't help but imagine the way he would feel around my dick.

"Are you imagining it's my cock?" I ask him, adding another finger, grazing the tips over his prostate. "Because I am."

"Please, Jordan," he whimpers. "Do that again. Please."

Fucking him with my fingers, I watch him writhe every time I hit that spot.

I couldn't wait for the day where he would be able to give all of himself to me, and I would greedily take all of him. Mine to hold. Mine to have. Mine to keep.

Keeping a steady pace, my free hand reaches for his cock, stroking him, from base to tip, spreading pre-come all up and down his length.

Gael's body bucks on the bed, eager and wanting. Torn between trying to thrust up into my fist, and push down onto my fingers.

"I'm going to come," he calls out. "I can't... shit."

"Come," I coax, working him over harder and faster, making sure he feels me everywhere. Making sure my hands ghosted his skin long after I'd touched him.

"Come for me," I growl. He groans loudly, his body arching up off the bed, his muscles straining against his skin as he shudders and spams through his release. "Fuck, you're so beautiful right now." His arousal coats my hand, his hole clenching around my fingers, and my cock aches in desperation.

"Oh my God, Jordan," he pants, sitting up on his elbows as I reluctantly move my hands away from him and trying to catch his breath. "That was incredible."

"You're incredible," I say, my eyes roaming up his body. I wrap my messy hand around my own stiff cock and stroke myself, even more turned on by the fact I'm rubbing his come all over my length.

Taking in his flushed skin and dilated pupils, we stare at one another as my hand moves up and down at a desperate pace. He looks perfect. Relaxed, blissed out, and so fucking content; nobody has ever looked sexier.

"I want to stay in here forever," I confess breathlessly. "You looking at me like that."

"You looking," he interrupts and gestures to me. "Like that."

I smirk. "Like what?"

"Naked, horny, frenzied." He rises up to his knees and wraps his arms around my neck. "I've been stealing glances at you for a really long time, but nothing could've prepared me for how fucking sexy you are like this." He glances down at my cock and back up at my face, lust and love blazing in his eyes. "It's a sight to see."

With my gaze never leaving his, my hand never falters. I stroke myself faster, my skin breaking out in goose bumps, and my body filling with heat. It's the perfect combination, as my balls tighten and my muscles coil in expectation.

With Gael's eyes on me, full of unquenched thirst, my need for release becomes uncontainable. "Kiss me," I demand gruffly, as my orgasm rushes through me and bursts out in an explosion of euphoria. "Fucking kiss me."

13

———

JORDAN

OVERWHELMED BY EMOTIONS AND FEELINGS, Gael and I shower in a loud silence, filled with soft, lingering touches, and our future at our fingertips. It's in the words that we don't say, that I feel the ten-year-old wall between us disintegrate into dust.

There's no such thing as time and space as we dry off and climb into the hotel bed, our bodies wrapped up around each other. Now that we've opened this door between us, the warmth and love are palpable. So much that it almost brings me to tears.

"I love you," I manage to say, no longer muffled out by the music in the nightclub or surrounded by unaware spectators. Now it's just me and him, and I have so much to say. Things I should wait to tell him, and things that I can't wait to tell him.

Untangling myself from him, I lay myself on top of him, nestling my body between his legs and resting my chin on his chest.

"I've always loved you, but saying the words out loud, to

you..." I blow out a loud breath. "It's so much more than I could've ever anticipated."

Gael runs his fingers through my hair, that look of complete contentment *still* on his face. "I know."

A small chuckle leaves my mouth, one filled with awe and disbelief. "Like, I'm ridiculously in love with you."

I feel his heart race underneath me as a wide smile spreads across his face. "I love you too. I love saying it to you, more than anything. That freedom to actually feel how I feel about you."

I crawl up his body, till my chest rests on his, and I bury my head in his neck, pressing my lips to his pulse. "I don't know if there's ever been a day since you've been in my life that I haven't loved you."

Fingers trace the length of my spine. "Did you ever think we'd get here?"

"No," I say honestly, grateful he can't see the serene expression on my face. "It still doesn't feel real. Like once we walk out of this room, it'll almost be like we made it up."

"It's real," he says, his voice soft but full of certainty. "I would never hurt you like that."

Swallowing hard, I raise my head to look at him. "Like I hurt you, you mean?"

"We both know it wasn't intentional."

"But look how many years we've lost. If I wasn't so scared, it could be us getting married now." I lower my gaze, instantly shocked at how easily the words came out.

Gael rests his fingers under my chin and tilts my head up. The adoration in his eyes has my heart expanding inside my chest. "I don't know what to do with myself when you look at me like that."

"I always look at you like this."

"No," I shake my head. "You don't."

It was like sitting in a dark football stadium at night, and seeing the shadows moving, but unable to make out the exact shapes and plays but then flood lights come on, and you can see *everything*.

There was nowhere to hide now.

"You would get married to me?" Gael asks, circling back the conversation, his knuckles now brushing up and down my cheek.

"I would marry you," I reiterate. "In a heartbeat."

Feeling the sharp sting of tears at the back of my eyes, I try to repress my emotions enough to get the words out. To tell Gael everything that's in my heart so when we return to Seattle, he doesn't need to wonder where I stand.

"I know we don't talk about this a lot," I start. "Well, *I* don't talk about this a lot, but as you know, growing up, my parents were cold in nature. They weren't affectionate, but that didn't mean they were mean. They were disciplined and obsessed with routine and sometimes a little absent."

For several seconds I let myself get lost in my past and remember the kid I was all those years ago. I had gravitated to Gael from the moment our kindergarten teacher assigned us to sit next to each other. And when we became close enough to hang out with one another outside of school, I remember never wanting to leave him or his house.

"I didn't have any siblings," I continue. "And for a very long time, I compared my family to yours."

"You've never told me that," he interrupts.

"It's embarrassing," I admit. "Because there's no comparison. It's apples and oranges. But for a while, I used to go home and think, why didn't I have what you had? And when I told them I was gay and they were so content to just throw me away, part of me didn't expect anything different. Almost like they had been waiting for a reason to cut ties with me."

My voice cracks as deep, secret confessions come pouring out of my mouth. "I told myself it had to be me. Like maybe there was nothing about me worth keeping or loving."

"Jordan." His voice is just above a whisper, wrapping me up in a protective blanket, his hand never leaving my face. "I know you know that isn't true."

My insecurities often don't let me believe it, but being around Gael and his family has always made me feel like there was a chance it wasn't.

"It's so very easy for me to be that detached cold person who is a replica of my parents. I'm actually like that with everybody but you and your family." An unreserved smile tugs at my lips when I think of them all, and Gael's mouth mirrors mine.

"What made you smile like that?" he asks.

"I can't help it when I think of your parents and siblings and the kids," I say. "In their own special way, every member of your family taught me the importance of love and the joy of having it." I drag myself up his body, every part of us aligning, my face hovering over his. "I want that with you, Gael. So, when I say that I want to marry you..." Pausing, my eyes drop down to his lips, instinctively licking my own, and back to his eyes. "That's exactly what I mean. The marriage, the family... that life. I only want it, if it's with you."

"God," he breathes, his voice shaky. "I want to give you that. I *really* want to give you that."

For the first time, I hear fear and nervousness in his

voice, as if the true magnitude of what this means for him and how this will change everything has really seeped in.

Resting my forearms on either side of his head, I press my lips to his softly, reverently, before I give him the option to break my heart. "I'm not going to say this more than once, because it is a complete contradiction to everything I've just said, and just how deep this goes for me. But I'm going to give you this one chance. One chance to back out and go back to the way it was before we got here. One chance to go back to *her*." Saying the words hurts just as much as it would if he made the choice, but I continue. "I will still be your best friend. I will still stand as the best man at your wedding. I will forget this whole thing ever happened, if you need me to."

My heart beats furiously in protest, but I wait, patiently, in complete silence.

Eventually, he responds. "You would do that for me?"

"I would *literally* do anything for you."

"I'm not backing out of this," he says. "I know you think—"

"I don't think anything," I interrupt. "I just don't want a crazy weekend, that we can easily blame on alcohol, to become a lifelong obligation you had no intentions of attaching yourself to."

He raises an eyebrow. "A crazy weekend? Really?"

"Come on, Gael," I say, a little exasperated. "You know very well you're the one making the sacrifice here. You're the one who stands to lose so much. So I'm giving you an out."

"I don't need an out. Better yet, I don't want it." It's his turn to kiss me now. Tender and devoted, Gael's kiss is full of promise. Full of hope. "It might be wrong, it might be bad timing, it might be the dumbest decision you and I have ever made, but I. Want. You."

————

THE MORNING COMES with a renewed energy and a calm that I can't ever remember feeling. Despite the late bedtime and early wake up, Gael and I both have an unmissable spring in our step. And if either Seth or Ray have noticed, neither of them have said a word.

Last night was exactly what I needed. The intimacy of our conversation was the confirmation I needed that we could do this. That we *would* do this.

Even though I was at least eighty percent sure he wouldn't back out when I gave him the option, the relief that, for once, I was the person that somebody chose, somebody's priority, had fireworks going off inside my chest.

Now the six of us are being driven to the race track in an Escalade provided by the hotel, and Gael and I are sitting at the very back, doing our damndest not to touch. He's only inches away from me, but even that is too much.

Grateful the heat in the car is high, I shift out of my jacket and let it rest in the empty space between us. Sneakily, I slide my hand underneath the thick material, hoping Gael notices my attempt at a subtle invitation.

When his fingers intertwine with mine, it takes everything I have not to meet his gaze.

Purposefully looking out the window, I listen as the car fills with voices and conversation. I fight the urge to turn and smile at him, because I'm certain my face can no longer hide my feelings.

After last night, the mask has not only been lifted, but it

doesn't even fit anymore. I feel like a different person. Shedding my old skin and starting a new chapter in my life.

We alternate between tracing shapes on each other's palms and holding hands as tightly and discreetly as possible.

It's probably the closest we'll be for a few hours, yet somehow, it's perfectly imperfect.

We manage to make it to the track with only a few knowing glances from Julian. When we get inside, I give the host my name and they take us down to our own private room that's decked out with drinks, finger sandwiches, and a range of hors d'oeuvres and overlooks the parked cars and the track itself.

"Wade and I never got this kind of treatment when we came here," Deacon says as he walks over to the floor-to-ceiling window, Julian behind him.

"Yeah," Gael says, staring right at me, his eyes dancing with mischief. "Jordan sure knows how to make a guy feel special."

Smirking at the hidden meaning, I give him an imperceptible shake of the head and then shift my focus to the host waiting patiently to give us all a brief rundown of how things will go.

"Hey, I'm Tim and I'll be your chaperone for today," he says. "The drivers will be here in just under an hour," he advises. "They'll give you a tour of the track and then it'll be the safety talk and then you'll be able to jump in the cars."

"I'm going to be really sad going home tomorrow," Ray says sarcastically as he picks up a napkin and a few mozzarella sticks. "I may just have to convince my wife that we need this boys' trip every year."

Chuckles echo around the room and Tim continues.

"You can come back to this area any time and food and drinks will be served for the duration. Alcohol will not be available till after the tour and the driving, unless you choose not to get in the car. If you choose to drink instead, I'll hand you a wristband that says so and the servers will know they're allowed to serve you."

He pulls a clipboard from under his arm and places it in the middle of a nearby table. "Here are waivers that you all need to sign. They list the process and the requirements and the risks. If you have any questions, please don't hesitate to ask them."

All six of us head in the direction of the table at the same time. Seth grabs the forms, taking one and passing them along with a box of pens.

Once we've all signed the dotted line, the next hour passes quickly and we've finished the tour of the premises. Soon enough, we're all helping one another put on helmets and Tim is pairing each of us with a driver.

Even though the track can have more than one car circling the circuit, the drivers insist on one at a time, for both safety and maximum optimization of the experience.

Happy and in agreement, we all watch as Gael, rightfully, jumps into the passenger seat of the McLaren first, full of adrenaline and enthusiasm.

We're all feeling it, and I'm momentarily grateful that it isn't just Gael and me getting something out of this trip. Everyone seems like they're enjoying each other's company just as much as the day out.

Staring at Gael and the car, the five of us watch as the driver revs up the engine continuously. The noise getting louder, amping up the excitement. With the window down and a glorious smile spread across his face, Gael gives us all a wink as the driver finally puts the car into gear and speeds off.

The air is cold and crisp, but the sun mixed with the excitement coursing through me provides enough warmth to take the edge off the winter day. Unbeknownst to everyone else, especially Gael, I paid for a few extra laps just to ensure he walks away having had the complete experience.

We're all watching and talking as Gael circles the track for a second time, the speed almost incomprehensible. I turn to the side to find Julian standing next to me, his hands shoved deep in his pockets.

"Are you okay?" I ask.

He nods. "I think Deacon might come in his pants right now, he's that excited."

I glance to find a usually serious and stoic Deacon excitedly talking to Seth and Ray, with his hands flying every which way as a means of explanation.

When I look back at Julian, he too is watching Deacon with a smile so wide, it lights up his whole face.

When Julian notices me watching him, he just shrugs. "I know, I'm ridiculously in love with him."

It takes me a split second to realize the usual pang of jealousy doesn't hit this time, the loss of such a heavy weight infuses me with unrestrained hope. "I love him too, you know?"

"I know you do." With both of us focused on the car roaring around the track, Julian nudges my shoulder, following my train of thought perfectly. "I know you do. I've always known you do."

"So who's going next?" Deacon calls out, interrupting any further conversation.

Dragging my gaze off Gael, both Julian and I look over

our shoulders in time to see three sets of eyes widen and look past us at the same time a loud screech of tires against asphalt pierces my ears. There's nothing but complete shock and horror on their faces, and by the time my brain processes where they're looking and who they're looking at, their devastated expressions confirm it.

Whipping my head around, my body stiffens, turning heavy and cold immediately.

I only looked away for a second.

The souped-up McLaren Gael is in, is spinning, a large plume of thick, white smoke building and rising, eventually enveloping the vehicle.

My eyes dart around the track, taking in the growing number of people gravitating to the scene. Trying to connect the dots, trying to predict a better outcome for Gael and the out-of-control car, and failing.

What is happening?

My gaze finally lands on the concrete barrier that surrounds the circumference of the track, at the exact same time the car does. Everything around me stops as I watch the McLaren crunch into the wall, the thunderous sound of the crash surrounding me, and the smell of burnt rubber filling my lungs.

"Gael," I scream, the sound of my voice loud and painful. "Gael."

As if I've been filled with lead, I try to move. Try to run to him, try to do anything, but I'm rooted to this single spot, wailing for him at the top of my lungs.

"Gael," I shout again, the harsh scratch against my vocal cords immediate. "I need to get to him. Gael."

"Jordan, calm down," a voice says into my ear, and that's when I notice Ray's big arms around me, pressing on my chest, holding me in place. "Breathe and let the medical team get to him."

Fear starts to thaw out the shock, and I can feel the panic setting in. "I can't breathe," I say quietly. "I can't breathe." When Ray's hold on me doesn't loosen, I begin gasping for air, my voice erratic, every part of me completely apart. "You have to let me go. I can't breathe."

"Let him go," Julian says, pushing past Deacon, Seth, and the instructors. "Let him go."

He stands in front of me, his brown eyes glassy, his cheeks red from the cold. He grabs my face, forcing me to tear my gaze off the mangled car. "Ray is going to let you go, we're going to wait for them to get him out safely and then we'll know more, okay?"

"I can't," I cry, my eyes wildly trying to look past Julian. "I just... we were supposed to..."

"I know," Julian nods. "And you will. Let's just deal with one thing at a time."

My mouth forgets how to work. All the words too much and too hard and not enough. I can't lose him before I've ever really had him. I can't. I refuse to.

"Let me go." Anger and adrenaline now giving me strength, I violently try to move out of Ray's returned tightened grip. "This wasn't supposed to happen," I manage through tears, talking to myself, not caring who hears me. "This wasn't supposed to happen. He has to be okay. He has to be okay."

"Are you the group here with Gael Herrera?"

We all look to see a wrung-out paramedic staring at us with nothing but sympathy in her eyes. "Are you his friends or family?" she asks again.

"His family," Seth says firmly. "How is he?"

"He and the driver are currently being taken to University Medical Center as we speak," she informs us.

"Is he alive?" I blurt out, asking the only thing that matters.

"Sir." Whatever it is she sees on my face has her softening and stepping closer to me as if I'm a caged animal she's trying to tame. She stares directly at me. "How about we get you all to the hospital first?"

14

———

GAEL

"I THINK I forgot to introduce myself out there," the instructor says. "My name is Matt." We both reach for the safety harnesses and secure them across our bodies. "It'll get harder to talk as we drive, but if you need anything just let me know."

"Thanks."

"Your friend paid for a few extra laps, so we'll be in here for longer than the original two."

"Why am I not surprised?" I say, more to myself. I didn't need to ask which friend he was referring to, because I knew there was only one man out there who was obsessed with spoiling me. "He's got a really bad habit of over-spending."

"This is totally worth it," he says, revving up the car.

Looking out the window, I find all of them staring at me, but I only have eyes for him. I've only ever had eyes for him. Without a care in the world, I wink at him. *I love you.*

There's something about moving at a ridiculously fast speed that makes you feel absolutely liberated. I may not be doing the hard work or concentrating on the actual driving, but for the first time in a long time, every part of me feels free.

As the speed of the car escalates, and my body leans and bounces with every slide and turn, my smile grows. I close my eyes, rest my head back on the seat and just let myself feel.

I'm happy and I can't find it in me to feel anything else.

Apart from Matt, I was by myself for the first time this whole trip. Me and my thoughts and everything that had taken place these last few days.

Every emotion, big and small, was floating around in my head and filling my heart. I had never realized how out of sync I was with myself. Through nobody's fault but my own, I'd thought I was happy, but this time with Jordan just proved that whatever I'd felt before this wasn't happy.

I'm well aware of how terrible that sounds and how unfair it is to Elena, but the hard truth is, this isn't about her.

She has done nothing but love me. Unconditionally. And the reality is, I love her, but just not enough. Not as much as she deserves and not in the same way I love Jordan.

And even though the love I have for him doesn't erase the shame and regret that comes with hurting her—because this whole thing *will* hurt her— I can't go back.

I can't pretend none of this happened; not like the first time we were in Vegas, and not like the first time we kissed.

None of us deserve to live in a lie, and I was finally coming to terms with that. Nobody won if I stayed with Elena while my heart belonged to Jordan.

It was one choice with three very different life-altering consequences.

And I didn't want consequences. I wanted endless possibilities. A future. A fucking happy ever after.

I wanted everything. With *him.*

I'm jolted out of my thoughts, my eyes flying open, when I feel the unwelcome sideways slide of the car as we take a turn. I fully expect the instructor to reposition the car, but when he oversteers and the vehicle continues at rapid speed to spin in a circle, I know things aren't looking good.

Turning to look at Matt, I watch his hold on the wheel tighten, his knuckles white and straining, and his legs trying to manage the clutch and the brake, as he tries to wrangle the car into some sort of submission. But every attempt at trying to regain control seems futile.

Thick, rubber-scented smoke from the tires starts to rise from underneath the car, blocking the view of my surroundings. The speed and direction of the car is no longer something I can measure by the whirl of the view around us, only feeling it as my heart races painfully inside my chest and my stomach dips as if I'm on a rollercoaster.

Matt is screaming words into his headset, but my brain can't put them together to make a sentence. Instead, I surrender to the imminent crash on our horizon, knowing logically there's no other way this car will stop, and beg my body and mind to relax. But no matter how hard I instruct my limbs to cooperate, it doesn't work. Every part of me is stiff. Every part of me is scared. Every part of me wonders if this is really how it all ends for me.

Running out of options, I choose to close my eyes and think of Jordan, and that hurts just as much as the impending impact. If this is life and death, I don't want to see my life flash before my eyes and focus on all the time I wasted being too scared to follow my heart. The years we didn't have and the years we were supposed to have.

I conjure Jordan up behind my eyelids, sketching the features of his beautiful face in my mind. Memorizing the way he looked at me this weekend when he told me he loved me. His smile. His eyes. His scent. His touch. *Him.*

Please, God, don't take all that away from me.

I beg and plead and pray.

This is supposed to be our time together.

I beg and plead and pray.

Matt's voice finally comes through and the words "Hold on, man, we're about to hit," register loud and clear.

My body flies forward, but the harness doesn't hold me back enough, and my body, along with my helmet-covered head, hits the dash before plunging back into the seat.

My ears ring, and my vision goes white before it goes black.

I can't see. I can't hear. I can't feel.

Jordan.

But I beg and I plead and I pray.

15

JORDAN

"JORDAN."

My bones tremor in my skin, from fear or from being cold, I can't tell. I've been sitting on these uncomfortable chairs, trying to channel my thoughts into something positive, but I have nothing.

Not a single doctor has come through to talk to us; only nurses able to tell us to wait and we will be notified as soon as possible.

Don't they know soon isn't soon enough?

I raise my head and find both Seth and Ray looking at me expectantly. They're standing side by side, exhaustion written all over their faces.

Ray holds up his cell. "I can't keep this from Laura any longer. And I don't know who his next of kin is. I can't have them calling Emilio and Maria and freaking them out."

I have to make a concerted effort to swallow past the sizable lump in my throat as I think of everybody back home. "I'm his next of kin," I tell them.

"You are?" he asks.

I shrug. "It was a while back. He didn't want anyone calling and scaring his parents."

It makes total sense considering Ray too was just worried about the same thing. If anyone is wondering why he never changed to Elena, they don't say a word about it.

"Okay, we have some coffees and sandwiches," Julian announces, he and Deacon returning from the cafeteria. "I don't know how good they are, but just try and eat or drink. We don't know how long we're going to be here."

My gaze lands on his, just as Seth says, "Can you call Elena?"

I flinch at his request, and Julian notices, his eyes full of sympathy and sadness.

Completely oblivious to my discomfort, I turn and nod at Seth. "Yeah, I'll call her now."

We're interrupted by a harsh swing of doors, the conversation immediately forgotten and all hope hinged on the doctor walking toward us.

"Is there a Jordan Varga out here?" she asks.

"Yeah." I cough to clear my throat. "Yeah. That's me."

"We've got you listed here as Mr. Herrera's next of kin."

"Is he okay?" I demand, the formalities so unnecessary. "We haven't been told a single thing. Is he alive?"

"Yes, he's alive."

My whole body sags to the floor, crouching with my head in my hands at the relief of hearing those three words. Images of the way the car looked after the crash made it almost impossible to think he would survive it.

"Mr. Varga." Unexpectedly, her voice is closer, and I look up to see her mirroring my position, her ocean blue eyes firmly locked on mine. "Mr. Herrera is alive, but he has sustained some significant injuries."

At this, my body stiffens. "What kind of injuries?"

She looks up and around at the four pairs of eyes staring down at us and then back at me. "Besides a broken arm, he took a serious hit to the head. Unfortunately, the airbag didn't deploy. The helmet protected him some, but the force of the collision was stronger. This has resulted in some swelling around his brain."

"Will the swelling go down?" I ask.

"We've currently put him in a medically induced coma with hopes that's what'll happen."

"And how long does that usually take?" Ray asks.

The doctor rises up to her feet, and I follow, making it easier for her to address everyone. "At this stage, we don't know. It can range from a few days to a few weeks, and it's just too early to tell."

"Can we see him?"

"He's in the ICU and will remain there until the swelling goes down and we decide to wean him off the anesthesia. Only two of you can visit at a time."

With a soft smile, she leaves the waiting room, and we're all left staring at one another in silence. There's so much to do, so many people to tell, and so much to organize, but none of us say a word and none of us move.

None of us can believe that any of this is real.

Ray's the first one to speak. "I'm going to have to call Laura and work out what she wants to do. They're all going to want to come here."

Without a word, I pull out my wallet and hand Ray one of my credit cards. "Whatever anyone wants or needs to get here, just use this."

"What the fuck?" he says, angrier than I expect, immediately putting me on edge. "I can take care of my family, man."

I launch into his face, unexplainable rage bubbling to the surface. "They're my fucking family too," I spit out.

Clenching his jaw, he hands the piece of plastic to Seth and steps back. "I got phone calls to make."

Seth glances between us and then slips my card into my coat pocket. "I'm going to call Mariana. You call Elena, get her down here as quickly as possible."

Fuck. Elena.

My eyes begin to fill with unshed tears, and I pinch the bridge of my nose to try and stop them. They're useless here. Tears won't change a single fucking thing.

"Jordan."

It's then I remember Julian and Deacon are still here.

"Yeah."

"What do you need us to do?"

Think. Think. Think.

I run my hand up and down my face and pull out the credit card I tried to give Ray and hand it to Julian. "We're supposed to check out tomorrow, but can you maybe call the Aria and see if they can extend our stay? Even if we have to move to another room."

"Yeah, of course. Do you need anything from the hotel?"

I shake my head. "I don't think so."

"Are you okay to call Elena?"

"Ha." I laugh humorlessly. "I don't have a choice."

Unable to look at the helplessness all over Julian and Deacon's faces, I angle myself so I'm giving them my back. Sticking my hand into my pocket, I drag my cell out and rip off the Band-Aid.

"Hello." Her greeting is curious, because I don't usually call her. "Jordan. Is everything okay?" When I don't answer, she persists. "You're scaring me, Jordan. What is it?"

"It's Gael," I say weakly. "He's been in an accident."

————

"MR. VARGA, we're ready for you to come in and see him now."

Bracing myself, I cover my face with my hands and take in a deep, shuddering breath.

You can do this. You can do this. You can do this.

From the corner of my eye, I notice Ray stand and Seth grip his forearm, stopping him. Grateful that one of them notices I want to do this alone, I follow the nurse and pray to the god the Herreras unconditionally believe in and beg him to make this all okay.

I don't let myself think of any other possibilities, because I refuse to believe that we will only ever have this weekend.

That I will live the rest of my life knowing how he feels and tastes and touches. To know what it's like to kiss him, to hear him say "I love you", just to know I can't ever have it again.

I wipe at my wet eyes as the nurse's steps slow down.

"Okay." She turns around to face me. "Just prepare yourself, he's going to look a little banged up, but I promise you he isn't in any pain right now and any scratches and bruises will be gone before you know it."

I nod, absently, and follow her inside. When my eyes land on his lifeless-looking body, the nurse's words of comfort and reassurance feel hollow and empty. Nothing could've prepared me for this.

"Gael," I whisper, my heart breaking as I take him in. My steps are small and soft, as if there is any chance I can wake him. I lower myself onto the edge of the seat beside the bed and put my hand gently on his wrist so I don't nudge the IV that's lodged in the top of his hand.

"Gael. Gael. Gael," I chant.

He has bruises underneath his eyes, stitches on his forehead, and there's an oxygen mask on his face. His skin looks pale and clammy, and they have his arm bandaged up and sitting across his chest in a sling.

He's battered and broken. His body is a mirror image for the way my heart feels as I watch the man I love lie there, hurt and helpless.

"Everyone's on their way here," I tell him, my voice shaking, not knowing if he can hear me, or if it even matters. "The kids are staying with Seth and Ray's parents."

"I need you to be okay." The sentence ends on a sob. "We all need you to be okay."

Resting my head on the bed, I close my eyes, just grateful to be by his side. When I called Elena and told her, she was frantic, and guilt and sympathy ate at me that I was here and she wasn't.

Just because the last few days had been ours and ours alone, it didn't change the fact that when Elena arrives, he will be back to being hers.

I have no real claim on him. No authority. No rights.

I will have to give up my access to him and share him with her.

Unexpectedly, someone touches my back, and I look over my shoulder to see the nurse. "Are you okay if someone else joins in your visit? The men outside are itching to see him."

I swipe my hand under my wet nose and nod at her. "Yeah, that's fine. I'll leave and they can come in two at a time. I'll come back when they're done."

Returning to my previous position, I lower my head back to the bed, my hand still on top of his.

I realize I haven't moved, when the sound of someone sniffling comes from behind me. Remembering the others want to see him, I scoot my chair back, but hands land on my shoulders, keeping me in place.

"We're not going to kick you out, bro." It's Seth. "We can rotate. There's no one here he would want by his side more than you."

His words hit my chest, seep past my skin, and settle around my heart, causing an unexpected flood of tears to run down my face. I can't control the crying, finding it even harder to stop.

I know, deep in my bones, it's the truth, but with everything going on in my mind, it's still hard to hear.

Seth doesn't move his hand off my back, but doesn't offer more comfort either. There isn't much more to be said. We're all stuck in limbo; a long waiting game with no solid end in sight.

"He's going to be okay." He tries for conviction, but the crack in his voice is too hard to hide. "He has to be. Mariana won't ever be the same."

I hear the words he doesn't say. I hear the truth that I don't want to acknowledge.

If something happens to Gael, none of us will ever be the same.

You can't turn the light off and expect to see.

You can't take away the flavor and still expect the food to taste good.

You can't live when you've lost purpose.

You can't love when your heart has stopped beating.

There is no Herrera family without Gael.

And there is no me without him.

I keep my head down, and the tears find their own rhythm and time to fall. Seth eventually leaves and Ray spends some time in the room. He tries to talk to me, but I'm too exhausted to offer more than a nod or the shake of my head.

By the time Julian and Deacon return from the hotel to take turns, I'm numb with exhaustion.

"Why don't we swap," Julian suggests. "You can go back to the room. Take a shower. Nap or change?"

My head snaps up with energy I wasn't aware I possessed. "No. I'm not going anywhere."

Not till Elena arrives, I tell myself.

Not till I have no other choice.

16

ELENA

TEARS SLIDE down my face as I stand in the doorway of Gael's hospital room. It's one thing to be told he's injured and sedated. It's another thing to see it in person.

I have no idea what I was expecting, but seeing his usually strong and robust body reduced to nothing in the too-small hospital bed wasn't it.

I had hoped Jordan's distress over the phone was a panicked, in-the-moment exaggeration; but this is worse than I anticipated.

This is the man I love looking like he's teetering on the edge between dead and alive.

My gaze moves to the other body in the room.

Jordan has his head buried in the crook of his arm, and his hand is tightly holding Gael's.

My eyes linger on the way he touches my fiancé, and I try to push away the jealousy, but it rears its ugly head at him being here this whole time with Gael instead of me.

It's irrational. They were away together. There was no way that I could get here any quicker than I did, but my gut churns with resentment anyway.

Finding the courage to step into the room, I wipe my tears and move toward the other side of the bed.

The empty chair scrapes obnoxiously against the linoleum, and Jordan's head jolts up, his red-rimmed eyes wide and unfocused.

"It's just me," I whisper, taking my seat.

He lowers his eyes to where his hand rests and then back to me. The guilt swimming in his gray-blue eyes is impossible to miss.

"Don't move on my account," I bite out.

His back straightens, the tired fog from earlier lifting. I have no idea where the harsh tone comes from, but the bitterness taking root in my stomach makes it difficult to regret my outburst.

I want to tell myself I'm being unreasonable, but his hand still hasn't moved, and everything inside me is screaming at me that the action alone means more than friendship.

It's always been more than friendship. It's always been *something*. Every part of me knows there's something unfathomable between them, and I still let my heart get away from me with Gael.

I've lived a life of second best. A life of not good enough. A life of wanting and craving more for myself, and somehow, I ended up exactly where I didn't want to be.

Giving my heart and my all to someone who wouldn't or couldn't do the same for me. The worst part is, even if he only loved me with half his heart, he loved me more and better than any other person ever has.

And his family. I am *so* in love with his family. They are the first real family I have ever had. Even Jordan and all his jealousy aren't enough to make me walk away.

When we found out we were pregnant, my world had

never felt so complete, and the happiness that had blossomed between us because of the news gave me security and certainty that pushed away those niggling doubts and ugly insecurities.

And yet, here I am, in a hospital, with no child, an impending wedding—happening because of a shotgun proposal—and a gut feeling that even in his weak, fragile state, I am losing the man I love to his best friend.

17

JORDAN

I WAS USED to sharing Gael with his family. Their closeness wasn't anything I had experienced before living with them, but now it was expected.

And with Gael in the hospital, it was no different. Eight adults filled the waiting room at any given time, with two of us coming and going from his room in a perfected rotation. Elena and his mom stayed beside him the longest, and I tried not to let the green-eyed monster show his ugly head.

There was a tension between Elena and me that neither of us could tame.

When she'd sat on the opposite side of the hospital bed, her eyes lingering on my hand over his, I felt like she could see right through me. And when her words hit me like the sharp flick of an elastic band on my skin, I knew it wasn't just a feeling. She fucking *knew*.

I couldn't talk to her and she wouldn't look at me. I had no idea if anybody else had noticed, but despite my desperate need to be by Gael's side for as long as I could, I knew I was the one who had to bow out.

Instead, I focused on the calm chaos of worry and love

that flowed between the family as we kept vigil for Gael. It had been a little over twenty-four hours since the accident, and much to everyone's relief, the doctors advised us that everything is healing according to plan.

Thankfully, the swelling on his brain is reducing at just the right pace. They're certain he will be dealing with the side effects of a concussion, but the severity of those side effects will only be determined by the cognitive tests conducted when he wakes.

So we all wait. Besides the few times we've taken turns to go back to our hotel rooms and shower, the hospital has become our temporary home.

It's my turn to go for the coffee run, so I quickly take everybody's order and head to the hospital cafeteria down stairs. While the food isn't the greatest, the coffee is good enough to keep each of us coming back.

As I step into the elevator, my cell rings in my pocket. I drag it out enough to see Frankie's name light up on the screen. Unsure if I'll have proper service, I let it go to voice-mail, planning to call him back later.

The doors open on the ground level and, just as I'm about to step out, I see Julian and Deacon walking toward me.

They both smile at me, but they look absolutely exhausted.

"Hey," we all say at the same time.

"How's it going?" Julian asks.

"There's talk that they're going to wake him up tomor-row," I inform them. "He's getting there."

Julian's shoulders sag and Deacon wraps a protective arm around him, doing anything in his power to make sure his husband knows he's always there for him.

"Have you guys considered going home yet?" I ask,

picking up on an earlier conversation the three of us had. "We don't know how long we're going to be here or when he'll be allowed to go home. I know you guys have jobs and lives to get back to."

The men look at one another, and I notice the change in their response to my suggestion.

"I feel guilty leaving," Julian says.

I shake my head. "Don't. He's going to know you were here and remember how we spent the time together before the accident, and you can catch up when he gets home. And I'm pretty sure Ray and Seth are heading back to Seattle to make sure the kids aren't out of their routine for too long."

"And what about you? Are you going to be okay if we leave?"

Before this trip, Julian and Deacon were friends of a friend, people who I know through Gael but wouldn't exactly call *my* friends.

But after everything we shared together, the way they had supported Gael and me and chose not to judge us, their decision to stay here at the hospital with us and be at everyone's beck and call when needed, that has definitely changed.

They were no longer just friends of a friend, and Julian's question, knowing he was referring to Elena being here, was confirmation. They were my friends now, my support system, people I knew without a shadow of a doubt I could call upon if I needed them.

Despite the jealousy and possessiveness that thrummed in my veins, my only priority was Gael being okay. It was the only thing that mattered.

Anything beyond that was selfish.

"I'm okay," I assure him. "Just one day at a time."

He nods softly. "We're going to go see him before we

head back to the hotel to pack up. Promise if you need anything, you'll call."

"I will. And in case I don't see you both before you go, thank you. For everything."

Julian is the first one to lean in for a hug, and I welcome the comfort. Deacon and I do a one-armed hug, and I watch them get into the elevator before walking the other direction to get the coffee.

When I eventually return with two trays of drinks, everybody is milling about in the waiting room. When I do a head count, I realize nobody is with Gael.

"Is everything okay?" I say as I reach them, trying to calm my frantic heart. "Why isn't anyone with Gael? Did something happen?"

Emilio walks over to me, taking a tray out of my hand and handing it to Mariana and then throwing his arm over my shoulder. "He's okay, *mijo*. They're just taking him for more scans to see if everything is on track. They will be doing more tomorrow, just to make sure all the details are in order before waking him up."

I sigh in relief. Everything is still going to plan. "I got coffee," I call out, feeling somewhat relieved. Mariana has already handed the ones on her tray out, but everybody else comes to me to get theirs.

Including Elena.

She reaches for her coffee, head down, refusing to look at me. Her name slips from my mouth before I even have a chance to think of what to say.

She reluctantly raises her eyes to meet mine.

"Are you okay?" I don't know why I ask her. It's not like I don't care, because I do. Of course I do. She loves him and she's hurting too, but the strain between us is too big. Too tangible. And neither of us can go back.

But I have to figure out how to make us move forward, because we can't be like this when he wakes up. And he's waking up. Soon.

Instead of answering me, she lifts the hot coffee to her mouth and takes a sip, her eyes never leaving mine.

I wait. And I wait. And all she does is turn and walk away.

————

AFTER ELENA IGNORED ME YESTERDAY, I left the hospital. It was the longest I'd stayed away, but I had no idea what to do with myself after that.

For several hours, I didn't want to play pretend, because I was sure I was going to have to put the mask back on that I'd taken off the night Gael and I kissed. And I didn't even know if I could make it fit anymore.

I told Seth to call me if anything changed, and I went back to the hotel room and lay down in the bed that Gael and I had slept on every night we were together.

Seth and Ray had moved to new rooms with their wives, closer to Emilio, Maria, and Elena, and I paid the overpriced daily rate just to stay here in a bed that I told housekeeping not to touch, because it smelled like him.

It was just me and him in here. The intimacy we'd shared, the love we'd declared. Our future plans. Our memories. And I didn't have to share any of these with a single other soul.

My cell chimes with a new text, and my hand darts out and around the mattress, looking for it immediately. I hadn't slept much, and now that the sun was finally out, I was grateful that I could stop trying.

My head is pounding, and I try to remember back to a

time where I didn't have a headache. The longer Gael is in the hospital, the longer the headache lingers.

I groan in frustration when I can't find the phone, sliding out of bed and shaking the blankets. I hear my cell land on the floor with a thud, and I drop the sheets in order to scour the area.

Finally finding it facedown underneath the bed, I flip it over and see a text from Ray.

Ray: Seth and Mariana are back at the hotel, asleep, but they told me to tell you if anything came up.

Even though I can see the three dots bouncing on the screen, I reply immediately.

Me: Did something come up?

Ray: I was supposed to text you earlier, but I got sidetracked FaceTiming the kids. They started weaning Gael off the anesthesia about two hours ago. They don't know how long it will take him to wake up on his own, but I figured you'd want to be here when it happens.

Well, yeah, I think to myself. I've already missed two hours. I tap at the screen a lot more aggressively than necessary.

Me: I'll be there soon.

In less than half an hour I'm showered and in an Uber, accompanied by a fresh-looking Mariana and Seth, on the way to the hospital. Nervousness and anxiety course through my veins.

I have no idea what to expect, but he's waking up soon, and with that, a seedling of hope begins to bloom inside my chest.

I try to pace my steps into the hospital, but I can't stop

myself from almost running. The doctors have advised us countless times that coming back to consciousness isn't instant. But I can't help but want to be there for every part of it.

When I make it to the neurological ward, Mariana and Seth in tow, we're surprised to find it empty. We head to Gael's room, finding it full with the rest of the family.

"Is he awake?" I ask, struggling to see past them.

"No," Laura says. "But the nurse said, if we were quiet, we could all be in here."

"But since nobody knows how to do that," Ray interjects, "I'm sure they're going to kick us out soon."

Laura glares at her husband, and that makes us all smile. "We just want him to know we're here and waiting for him."

"Actually, Jordan, I'm glad you're here." Ray turns to me, his expression serious, the mood changing quickly. "Can we have a talk outside for a second?"

Nodding, I follow him into the hallway, not really sure what to expect. "What's up?"

"Laura and I have been talking with Mariana and Seth, and we think it's a good idea if we all go home after Gael wakes up."

I tilt my head to the side. "I'm not sure I'm following."

"Providing that everything goes okay when he wakes up, the four of us are going to go back to Seattle, and Emilio and Maria are coming with us," he explains. "They're not going to let him out immediately, and I don't even know if they're going to let him fly home. And we feel shitty doing this... hell, we all hate having to leave at all, but the kids—"

I raise my hand up to cut him off. "You have nothing to feel guilty about. None of you. This isn't easy, and the kids need you all just as much."

"So you'll stay here, with Elena? Help her bring him home?"

Only an idiot would have trouble following where this conversation was going, yet the request still catches me off guard, and not for any of the obvious reasons.

I wasn't leaving Vegas without him. Everybody knew that, but could Elena and I put everything aside to get him home in one piece?

How would *he* feel being confined with both of us, after everything that happened?

My options were limited, and my delay in answering was confusing Ray, because even though he was asking me for a favor, the expectation for me to comply was still very much there.

Despite the turmoil rolling around in my gut about the execution of this whole thing, I nod and agree, because this isn't about Elena and me. The priority is, and always will be, Gael.

Ray claps me on the shoulder, giving it a squeeze. "We're all so lucky to have you in our family, man. I don't know if we tell you enough."

The acknowledgement and praise hit hard and fast, and the mixed bag of emotions I've been carrying around for the last few days has the backs of my eyes stinging.

They're always thanking me, and I never get tired of hearing it, but the truth is, I'm the one who's lucky. I'm the one who's forever thankful to each and every one of them.

Words fail me, so I place my palm over his hand and hope the simple gesture conveys my gratitude.

Silently, we walk back into Gael's room, and Maria turns to us, a smile I haven't seen in days stretching across her face. "He's waking up, *mijo*."

Already?

18

GAEL

VOICES. Why can I hear voices?

Quiet murmurs and whispers continue to hum around me, but I can't seem to work out who it is or where it's coming from.

I try to open my eyes, to find out who's talking, but my lids are heavy, like lead, refusing to open.

I try again and... nothing

Why can't I open my eyes?

The hushed voices become a little louder this time, like every other one of my senses is compensating for my lack of vision.

"Gael, *mijo*, take your time. We're all here waiting. There is no rush."

My mother's voice is unmistakable, but what is she talking about? Who's waiting? And for what? And why is my head throbbing?

Concentrating hard, I try again, and still... nothing.

"It's okay," she coos. "You'll be okay."

Confused by her words, I feel my breathing start to change, the pace quickening, my breaths shortening. A loud beeping sound pierces through my ears, making my temples pound harder. I try to take a deep breath, but the suction-like feeling over my nose and mouth has my heart racing and panic setting in.

Am I in a hospital?

I attempt to raise my hand to my face, and I'm struck with an awful searing pain in my arm.

At this point, my determination overpowers the pain, and I force myself to push past the heaviness and the headache and open my eyes.

But it seems I'm no match.

Once.

Twice.

On the third attempt, I feel a soft, delicate hand squeeze mine and a soft whisper in my ear. "You're doing so good, baby." It's Elena. She's here. "You've got this."

It must be obvious to them that I'm struggling, their words trying to encourage me and make me feel safe. But at this point, all it's doing is freaking me out.

It's obvious something's wrong. Something's clearly happened, but I can't figure out what. I keep my eyes closed on purpose now, too exhausted to even try again.

An unfamiliar voice penetrates through my confusion and the sound of footsteps comes closer. A cold hand lands on my upper arm. "Gael, honey, my name is Magda. I'm your nurse. You were in a car accident and hit that head of yours. Your mom is holding your left hand, and I want you to give it a little squeeze if you can hear me."

I follow her exact instructions.

"Excellent," she praises. "I'm going to ask a few more questions, you just squeeze your mom's hand if the answer is yes."

I tighten my grip on my mother's fingers and she chuckles softly. *"Vas muy bien, Gael."*

"Now, Gael," Magda starts. "Are you in pain?"

I think of my arm and my head. On instinct, my mouth opens and the word comes out just fine. "Yes."

Why didn't I think to speak before?

The sound of my voice is hoarse, thick, and unused.

"Well, look at that," the nurse says cheerfully. "Do you think you can try and open your eyes again?"

"Again?" I ask with confusion.

"You've been waking up on and off for a few hours now, and you opened your eyes for a few seconds the last time."

"I don't remember that."

"That's normal."

With a shaky breath, I try again. And this time, my eyes cooperate. It's slow and slight, but they open enough that the halogen light shining in the room makes me squint.

"Why does that hurt so much?" I ask, closing them again.

"Let's concentrate on one thing at a time," she advises. "Opening your eyes, measuring your pain level, then we'll talk."

She had only listed three things, but it all already felt like too much. I open my eyes again, this time trying harder to keep them open, allowing the blur of the room to finally come into focus.

My gaze moves slowly around the room, meeting my mother's tired and weary eyes, then my father's matching pair, and finally Elena's.

She looks wrecked.

Her eyes have lost their sparkle; they're now tired and rimmed with dark, sunken circles. Her lips are cracked from all the biting I know she does when she's stressed, and her nose is red and dry, clearly from crying.

She looks like she's been to hell and back because of me, and yet my brain and thoughts are too foggy to make sense of how I got here. I take inventory of my body, mentally cataloging every move I make.

Apart from a sluggish, tired feeling, my feet and legs fare fine. One of my arms is clearly broken, resting across my chest in a cast and a sling. And my head. It feels like it's going to explode. If it weren't being held up by the bed, there's no way I could manage it on my own. Add the pressure behind my eyes, and I was wondering how soon I could go back to sleep.

"What happened?"

Elena leans forward, but my mother surprises me by abruptly cutting her off. "We'll let Jordan explain it to you, *mijo*. He was there."

Jordan.

My heart skips a beat at the mere mention of him.

"Is he hurt?" My eyes close of their own volition, the thumping in my head somehow more pronounced and too much to deal with at the idea of Jordan being injured too.

"No. He's okay," my dad answers. "You just worry about yourself right now."

"Okay," the nurse interrupts. "How's the pain?"

I half open one eye. "You mean my head?"

"The one and only."

"It's pretty bad," I say honestly.

"That's to be expected." She offers me a sad smile. "I'm going to check all your vitals, give you some medication for your head, then call the neurologist to come and discuss the injury with you. Until then, take it easy and close your eyes and rest. And remember"—she reaches for a pen in her

breast pocket and points at each of my family members—
"no more than three people in here at a time. I don't want to
have to kick some of you out like before."

Propping my head in a more comfortable position and
closing my eyes, I ask, "There are more people here?"

"Yes," Magda answers while wrapping the blood pressure cuff around my arm and clipping the pulse oximeter on
my finger. "You are one loved man."

I hear the scratch of the pen running across paper
before she says. "Your blood pressure and pulse are good.
Some food and water will make them even better, but it's
normal to not feel hungry straight away." She rids me of the
medical paraphernalia. "I'll be back with some ibuprofen
and then I'll be out of your hair."

Anxious to know more about what happened, but
feeling my energy being depleted by the second, I open my
eyes and slowly turn my head to look at Elena.

"Can you get Jordan in here please? I want to know
what happened."

———

I HADN'T REALIZED I'd fallen back asleep, but the addi-
tional medication the nurse provided me after the ibuprofen, hit me hard. This time the wake up is a lot less painful
and dramatic than the one before. I open my eyes, hoping to
see Jordan, but make sure my disappointment doesn't show
when I see Mariana, Seth, Laura, and Ray sitting on either
side of the bed.

"I thought only three of you were allowed at any given
time," I joke groggily.

Mariana slaps a hand over her mouth as tears fall down
her face and she stifles a sob.

"Hey," I say, trying to soothe her. "I'm okay."

Every part of me wants to reach over and comfort her, but I just don't have the physical energy to do anything other than lie here helplessly.

Seth wraps her in his arms, pulling her closer to him, and despite my personal confusion, I'm so relieved to know they've all been here, dealing with this together.

I angle my head to look at Ray and Laura, and she's silently crying too as she leans on his shoulder.

"Where's Jordan?" I ask again, remembering I wanted to see him before I fell back asleep. "I want to know what happened."

"You don't remember the accident?" Seth asks incredulously.

"No," I tell him. "I can't remember how I got here. At all."

"We were there," Seth continues, gesturing between him and Ray. "Both of us with Jordan and Deacon and Julian."

Deacon and Julian were here?

Before I have time to process my confusion, Jordan stands in the doorway, leaning on the frame, his hands buried in his pockets. Just like everyone else, the toll the accident has taken on him is unmissable. My pain and injuries are physical and obvious, but with his gaunt cheeks, unshaven face, and desolate stare, he just looks haunted.

"Are you coming in?" I manage to ask.

Four heads turn to the doorway.

He forces a smile. "I'm just trying to wait for my turn."

"Well, we have to get going anyway," Seth advises. "We have to get back to the kids and we have flights to book."

I scrunch up my face. "Flights? Why do you need flights?"

Jordan pushes himself off the doorjamb immediately, stepping farther into the room.

"What do you mean, why do they need flights?" he asks, his voice almost harsh.

Before I get the chance to explain, an older, balding man enters the room, heading straight for me. The rest of my family rises off their chairs and signals that they'll wait outside, only Jordan remaining behind.

"Gael, it is so nice to see you awake. I'm Dr. Singh, your neurologist, and I just want to run over a few things with you. Hopefully, we can get you back home to Seattle within the next two weeks, if things are looking good."

His tone is chipper and positive. Reassuring even, until my mind snags on two of his words. Home. Seattle.

"What am I missing?" I ask, my heart rate picking up in panic.

The doctor reaches for his medical light and shines it at my eyes, stretching each of my eyelids up, trying to get a better view of my pupils.

"Your pupils look good," he announces. "Your vitals are great and the most recent scans we did confirm a severe concussion, but the swelling you inherited from the hit has decreased significantly."

He slips the mini flashlight back inside his pocket just as Elena walks into the room. She slips past Jordan, and I don't miss the twitch in his jaw as she takes a seat beside me and slips her hand into mine.

She glances at Dr. Singh. "Sorry. I wanted to be here to hear what you had to say."

"Of course. A fiancée always needs to know what's going on with her fiancé." He focuses back on me. "Okay. Now, I'm going to ask you a few questions and then we can start making sense of everything."

I nod.

"What's your full name?" he asks.

"Gael Herrera."

"How old are you?"

"I'll be thirty-one on June 11th."

"Perfect," he praises. "Now, tell me the names of the people in your family."

"Maria is my mom, Emilio is my dad. Mariana and Laura are my sisters, their husbands are Seth and Ray, their children are Sara and Nico, Alejandro and Lucia. And there's my fiancée Elena and best friend Jordan."

"Brilliant," Dr. Singh praises. "Now some hard ones. Do you remember the accident?"

My eyes dart between Jordan and Elena as I shake my head.

"Do you know how long you've been here?"

Another shake.

"Okay." Dr. Singh tries again, his voice now softer. "What is the last thing you remember?"

At this I stop. I know who I am. I know who everyone else is, but the other stuff feels impossible. Like it's just at the edge of my mind and I can't reach it.

"I don't know," I confess, emotion building up in my throat.

"Do you know where you are?"

"In a hospital?" I answer wearily.

"We're in Las Vegas," Jordan blurts out.

Dr. Singh looks over his shoulder, clearly giving Jordan a look he doesn't appreciate, because Jordan huffs and folds his arms across his chest.

"As Mr. Varga stated, Gael, you are in Las Vegas and you were in a car accident after you and your friends went drifting on one of Vegas's most popular race tracks."

His words fade into the distance as my mind scrambles for the memory.

I still come up empty.

"Is this normal?" I ask.

"Yes." He rises up off his seat. "Forgetting the accident is very common after a traumatic brain injury. It's called retrograde amnesia."

"Will I ever remember it?"

"You may," he says casually. "But you also may not. Since you remember very specific and important details, I would say the other stuff will fall into place over time. While there is no guarantee that any specific memory will be remembered, we also can't pinpoint, besides the accident, what it is exactly that you've forgotten. At this stage, the most important thing is your recovery." He glances at Jordan and Elena and then back at me. "Traumatic brain injuries are no joke. Concussions are no joke. And when I say he needs to take it easy, I mean Take. It. Easy."

He starts ticking things off his fingers. "Be prepared for pain when it's loud. Pain when it's too bright. Potential mood swings. Your ability to concentrate will be different to what it was prior to the accident."

"I'm a teacher," I blurt out, surprising myself but feeling relieved that I remember. "What about work? When can I go back?"

"I will be referring you to a neurologist in Seattle. Until your first appointment there, at which they will advise when you can return, you will not be working."

I sink deeper into the bed, all of it too much, the dull ache in my head returning.

"And when can I get out of here?" I ask dejectedly.

"Providing the scans continue to show progress, I think we may be able to set you free in two days."

"Can he fly?" Elena asks.

"At this stage, with a medical certificate that requires the airline to provide you with a wheelchair and allow you to have priority seating, I don't see a reason why not. Gael," he addresses me, his voice firm and expectant.

I open my eyes.

"Please be sure to let me know if any of your symptoms change. For the better or for the worse."

Nodding, I watch him exit the room, giving Jordan the space to come sit on the opposite side of Elena.

It was the first time he'd been near me since I woke up, and shame washed over me, because as my fiancée sat next to me holding my hand, I had missed him the most.

"Are you going to tell me what happened or not?"

19

———

JORDAN

IF I DIDN'T LAUGH, fake or not, I would either cry or scream, and I couldn't do either.

Gael wanted me to tell him *everything*, but the only things I wanted to tell him weren't options.

Not in front of his fiancée. Not at all.

Everything that'd happened between us. Everything we said. Everything we did. Everything we shared... it was now nothing more than a memory; one I couldn't ever forget, and one he may never remember.

I was vibrating underneath my skin, filled with an irrational amount of anger and guilt that was making me feel nauseous.

How the fuck did we get here?

I was past the sadness and the worry, and the relief that he was awake felt like it had been taken away from me more quickly than it was given.

It was such a selfish thought, to care about my feelings when he could've easily lost his life or suffered an irreversible brain injury.

I should have been nothing else but grateful, but I was sitting here like the third fucking wheel, again, and it fucking hurt.

Heaving a sigh, I scrub a hand over my face and will myself to suck it up.

This isn't about you Jordan. Not now.

"What is it exactly that you want to know?" I ask him.

"Why are we in Vegas?"

"Jordan organized it," Elena answers. "Organizing your bachelor party was his Christmas gift."

"Bachelor party," he echoes. He then turns to Elena. "What month is it?"

"It's January 5th," Elena tells him. "You were in Vegas for New Year's."

"So it's January twenty twenty-one." We both nod at him. "And we're getting married in March, right?"

Of course that's something his brain managed to retain.

She surprises me when she says, "If you're feeling up to it, but we can move it if we need to." She gives me a quick glance. "We also don't need to talk about it right now."

Ain't that the fucking truth.

"Just take it one day at a time," she says. "There's no rush."

"She's right," I add. "The only priority is you getting back home and getting back on your feet."

"Elena," he says, his tone serious. "Can you give us a moment?"

Dormant butterflies begin to flutter in my stomach, only to lose their flight when I hear him say, "I want to ask Jordan about the accident and I don't want you to hear anything that'll upset you."

"Do you really think that's a good idea?" I ask him. "Because knowing won't make a single bit of difference."

"But it might trigger a memory," he insists.

I, more than anybody else, wanted him to remember the last week and any other memories he had lost, but I didn't want to relive his accident. The fear I felt. How bad the car looked... it was a real-life nightmare.

"I know it's a lot to ask," he says, looking between Elena and me. "But I really need this."

Blowing out a breath, I roll out my shoulders. "Just the accident?" I confirm.

He nods. "For now."

Elena doesn't argue with Gael, but I catch the reluctance in her steps as she heads toward the exit.

"You didn't have to ask her to leave."

"She doesn't need to hear how I almost died," he says flatly. "Nobody does."

"But you want me to relive it?" I ask, voicing my discomfort.

"I would do it for you."

He doesn't say anything more, the simple statement saying enough.

"Fine." I scoot my chair closer, wishing I could hold his hand while I break my heart for what feels like the hundredth time.

As requested, I stick to only the accident, how it was something I had booked, and that we were each assigned a car with an instructor, but we weren't all going to be in the cars and on the track at the same time. Naturally, since he was the guest of honor, he went first.

"And then what happened?"

"Honestly, I don't know. One minute we were all talking and watching you speed past us, and the next, the car was spinning out of control. Your driver couldn't stop it, so you had to wait to hit something for the car to actually stop."

"Is the driver okay?"

"A little bruised, but his airbag reduced the impact like it was supposed to." He screws his face up in confusion, and I clarify. "Yours didn't. That's why you got hurt so badly."

"Does my face look terrible?" he asks.

Staring at him, my eyes dart around the bruises and scratches on his face, itching to skim my fingertips over every temporary imperfection. "You've looked better."

A half-hearted chuckle slips from his mouth as he glances at me, his features softening and eyes glassy. "I can't stand not remembering."

This time, I do cover his hand with mine, the need to comfort him outweighing anything else.

"I wish you could too," I say truthfully and selfishly. "But you're alive and healthy, and that's all that matters."

He slides his fingers in between mine, in a way we had never done before Vegas, and I had to wonder if he knew he was doing it and how familiar it felt.

Whether there was a method to his madness and continuously talking about the things he couldn't remember actually worked, I didn't know, but I wasn't going to be the one to let go of his hand first.

"It's amazing how tired I feel after a bit of conversation," he states.

"You should rest. We have plenty of time to catch up. And I know your family is going to want some extra time with you before they leave."

"You're staying, right?"

His gaze flickers down to our clasped hands and back up at me. His eyes are hazel pools filled with longing, and even though I didn't think he knew exactly what he was longing for, it seems he wasn't even trying to hide it anymore.

"I'll be here," I assure him. "I'll always be here."

———

THE SOUND of my cell ringing has me running out of the hotel room bathroom with nothing but a towel on. When I see Elena's name on the screen, I start to panic.

"Hello," I greet in a rush. "Is everything okay?"

"Hey. Yeah, it's fine, I just…" She pauses. "I just wanted to know if you needed help packing Gael's stuff. Or picking an outfit for him to wear home."

I had forgotten that everything he came to Vegas with was in this room. Seeing as I'm not the messy type, his clothes have already been folded in a pile beside the suitcase, and I was more than capable of picking out something for him to wear.

"It's fine," I tell her. "I can easily do all that."

"I'll just wait for you in the lobby then."

"Okay. I'll be down soon." An uncomfortable silence lingers before I add, "Bye."

Gael was finally being released from the hospital today. It was a day later than predicted, and it meant an extra twenty-four hours of Elena and me tiptoeing around one another, hoping Gael didn't notice. It was awkward and painful, but I knew we both loved him enough to do it again if we had to.

After the rest of the family had said their final goodbyes and headed back to Seattle, Elena and I did a damn fine job of playing nice in front of Gael. If it weren't for the fact that we were no longer keeping vigil and the doctors made us leave when visiting hours were over, neither one of us would've left his side.

We spent the days in his hospital room, keeping him company, and we spent the nights alone in our hotel rooms, pretending the other didn't exist.

For Gael, I wanted to be nice and accommodating and help her out if she needed it, but then I thought of how she got to hold his hand for eight hours straight, or how she had the freedom to kiss him on the lips and forehead whenever she felt like it, and the tension between us would seesaw from a simmer to a boil and then back again.

It wasn't until after lunch yesterday, when Gael uncharacteristically lost his cool with Elena for no reason, that the reality of his brain injury really hit home.

The doctor had mentioned mood swings as a side effect, but to see it in action had me hurting *for* her. He'd never spoken to anyone like that, and the way Elena curled into herself had me mad at Gael for the first time in a long time.

I tried harder after that, to get out of my own head and be nicer to her. To help her instead of hate her. Gael was the focus, and my feelings toward Elena were just an excuse to let myself get sidetracked and blame someone else for something that was out of both our control.

She would never say it, and I didn't expect her to, but I knew she appreciated it. The whole situation was new and different and uncharted, and we needed to start taking the advice we were dishing out to Gael, and take one day at a time.

I knew it wasn't a foolproof plan, and I knew my broken heart would try often to take the lead, and her broken heart would push me away, but I would at least try. Because helping her meant helping him.

Once I finished drying off after my shower, I got

dressed, picked an outfit and shoes for Gael, along with putting the stuff he might need on the plane in a backpack, and finished filling up our small suitcases.

It felt wrong to say goodbye to this room and to close the door on all our secrets and confessions. It was the only tangible proof I had of what we'd shared and the future we'd planned.

After the whole ordeal, this room had become my sanctuary. These four walls held every truth, every vow, and every sin we shared.

Leaving it felt like I was leaving him and giving up on us.

It was irrational, but there was nothing about us that was rational, normal, or logical.

My cell rings again, and when I see Elena's name come up again and the time, I know I've stayed up here too long.

"I'm coming," I say, in place of answering. "Sorry, I got held up."

"That's okay. I just don't want us to be late for our flight. We don't know how efficient the airport staff are going to be with all the paperwork."

"You're right," I agree. "I'll be down in a few minutes."

This time, I don't allow myself to look back, both literally and metaphorically.

By the time I check out, settle the bill, and hop into an Uber with Elena, the desire to be home in Seattle is overwhelming.

And when the doctors sign off on all of Gael's paperwork and give us permission to finally leave the hospital, I think all three of us have to stop ourselves from crying.

"I can't believe I'm leaving the hospital right now," Gael says as we pass through the automated doors, Elena pushing his wheelchair, me walking beside him. "I could do without the wheelchair, but this feels surreal."

"Are you in any pain?" I ask, ignoring his comment about the chair. "I bought you a hat and a pair of sunglasses from the hotel gift store in case the glare is too much."

"You did?" Elena asks, the disappointment that she wasn't the one who had thought of the small gesture was unmistakable.

I don't know why I do it, but I lie to make her feel better. "One of the nurses gave me the idea the other day. No big deal."

"Do you have them on hand?" Gael interjects. "Because this hurts way more than I anticipated."

"They're in the bag."

He looks down at the backpack I'd put on his lap and manages to unzip it and get what he needs from inside.

The car that'll take us to the airport is already waiting, and Gael's excitement shows as he slowly rises up off the chair. He reaches for the passenger seat and I put my hand on his forearm stopping him.

"The back is better for you," I advise. "You might need to lay your head down during the drive."

His eyes narrow at me, making his whole face scowl, the look I've very quickly started to associate with his dislike for being told what to do. It isn't intentional anger at Elena or me, but his mind keeps forgetting that it's healing and some things aren't the same.

It's not permanent, but he just can't seem to remember that.

"Don't give me that look," I chide. "Elena and I did some reading about concussions and what to expect and how to handle it. It just means you'll hopefully get back to normal quicker."

I can't see the roll of his eyes behind his glasses, but I feel it all the same. He and Elena slide into the back seat while I push the wheelchair back inside the hospital.

The drive to the airport is only fifteen minutes, but we've got enough time to find a wheelchair, check in, and head to the correct gate.

I let Elena handle talking to the airline staff, despite the need to want to be his only caretaker. I sit down on the bank of chairs and pull out my cell.

I text an update to Mariana and Laura, letting them know we've arrived at the airport and that I'll tell them when we land.

Then I pull up Frankie's number and hit call.

"God, you're a hard man to get a hold of," he says when he answers.

"Well, hello to you too."

"Where have you been? You were supposed to be at work days ago."

Everyone in the office knew I was out of town for Gael's bachelor party, but instead of telling them why I had extended my time off, I rearranged my schedule in the hospital waiting rooms and just sent out a vague email delegating new points of contact if necessary. Staff were only to call me if it was urgent, and Frankie had been the only one to do so.

Except his voice messages were more along the lines of "call me," "why are you ignoring me?" and "don't be dead."

"Is everything at work fine?" I ask.

"Of course it is, you know that's not why I called you."

Even though we use one another for sex for all the wrong reasons, Frankie's heart has always had the most honest intentions.

"Is everything okay?" he prods.

My eyes dance around the airport, stopping on Gael and Elena at the customer service desk. With him in a wheelchair, he was the perfect height for her to have her hands all over him. Touching his shoulder, his neck, his hair. "Gael was in a serious car accident."

"In Vegas?"

"Yeah. We've been down here since, but we're at the airport now, boarding soon to come home."

"Is he alright?"

"It's complicated," I offer vaguely.

His voice evens out, a little more serious, a lot more feeling. "Are *you* alright?"

I was trying so hard to be, but I felt like I was on the same rollercoaster of emotions Gael was on, having the same difficulties keeping them in check.

Frankie knew what Gael meant to me. It was the biggest point of contention between us, and yet I felt his genuine concern in the simple question.

"Yeah, I'm fine," I croaked out. "I'll be fine."

"Oh, babe," he whispers.

And the tenderness in his tone makes me want to bawl.

"How about I come over tonight?" he suggests. "After work?"

"Um, I don't think I can—"

He cuts me off. "Not for sex, you idiot. I gave my dick very clear instructions on Christmas Day, thank you very much."

A wet, throaty chuckle leaves my mouth. "I'm honestly fine. You don't have to check up on me."

"I'll see you later tonight," he insists. "Anything you want me to bring?"

"Frankie."

"I'll bring some dinner," he continues, completely

ignoring me. "If you need anything else between now and then, let me know."

"Frankie," I warn.

"Have a safe flight, Jordan, and I'll see you soon."

The line goes dead before I can answer or object, and I drag the cell off my ear and sigh.

Fucking Frankie.

20

JORDAN

JUST AS I slip the fresh t-shirt over my head, the doorbell rings.

When I open up to see Frankie on the other side, holding a pizza box, I'm surprised by the smile that tugs at my lips.

"Hey." I step back, opening the door all the way. "Come in."

He saunters in, still in his pressed pants and blazer from work. Heading straight for the kitchen, he puts the food on the counter, opening the box and grabbing clean plates and napkins from a nearby cupboard.

"What are we drinking?" he asks as he opens the fridge. "Wine or beer?"

"You do know I can get the drinks in my own house?"

I drag a stool from under the kitchen counter and take a seat, watching him fuss over me in my own house.

Truth be told, I'm too tired to argue with him.

Now, showered and unpacked, the surge of caffeine and adrenaline had well and truly left my system. And I was beat.

He hands me a beer and then takes a seat opposite me.

"How's work?" I ask.

"That's not what I came to talk about and you know it." He picks up a slice of pizza and puts it on his plate. "Do I need to plate yours too? Maybe feed you with my hands?"

"Shut up," I say with a chuckle. I reach for my beer and take a long pull. "Thank you." I point the bottleneck at the food. "You didn't have to do this."

"Stop stalling and tell me what happened." He takes a sip of his own beer and I choose that exact moment to say, "He was going to leave her when we got back, but he hit his head in the accident and now he doesn't remember."

Frankie chokes on the liquid, spraying it all over his pizza and the counter. He slaps at his chest as he tries to regulate the coughing and the choking.

"Jesus. Fuck." He continues to cough. "You weren't kidding. How bad was the accident?"

A shiver races through me as the image of the wrecked car, and Gael inside of it, pops up in my memory.

"I was sure he was dead," I tell him. A thought I had been too scared to voice at the time in case it came true. "They put him in a medically induced coma for two and a half days, and when they woke him up, he didn't remember a thing. Didn't know we were in Vegas, didn't remember it was his bachelor party, and sure as fuck didn't remember telling me he was in love with me."

His gaze darts between me and the pizza. "We really should've eaten first because this food is definitely going to get cold now."

I chuckle. "If I remember correctly, I did ask you how work was. But it's fine, you eat and then we'll talk."

"You're not going to eat?"

"Honestly, I haven't been able to eat properly since it happened."

"In that case, I'm leaving you leftovers." He grabs a new slice that doesn't have beer drizzled all over it and brings it to his mouth. "I'll eat. You talk."

And that's what I do. I unload a whole week's worth of emotions and misfortunes and heartache onto Frankie's shoulders because I'm already too damn tired and they're too damn heavy to carry them on my own.

By the time I'm finished telling him about what happened with Gael and then what happened with Elena, we're both sitting in recliners, each with beers in our hands.

"And you don't want to tell him?" he asks hesitantly.

"It feels so selfish to tell him," I say, admitting that the thought had crossed my mind. "He's got a good four to eight weeks of recovery ahead of him before his life is any semblance of normal. I don't want to complicate it even more."

Frankie reaches over his chair and puts his hand on my forearm. "But you said he admitted to always loving you. If he can remember things before the accident, then that hasn't changed."

I knew Frankie was right. I'd felt our connection, even when he was too confused in the hospital to acknowledge what it was himself. But was I going to make him admit to cheating on his fiancée at a time like this? Was I going to add the stress of having to tell her and cancel their wedding at a time like this?

Tilting my head back on the recliner, I close my eyes and let out an exhausted sigh. "I really don't know. I want to be there for him. With every fiber of my being, I do want to be there for him, but I can't watch her with him. I have spent years pushing down what I feel for him, trying to ignore it. But I can't do that now."

Not when I know what he really wants, what his heart really desires. How was I supposed to go on forgetting any of this ever happened?

"I just don't know where to go from here," I say truthfully.

"I'm thinking your life would've been a whole lot easier if you fell in love with me."

Smiling, I open my eyes and angle my head to look at him. "You would have to be in love with me too for that to work out, and we both know you're as emotionally unavailable as I am."

"I try more than you do," he argues. And he does. We both tried to be something more, but I'm pining for something I can't have and he's just trying to fill the empty void in his heart that someone left behind.

"Thank you, Frankie."

He picks at the label on his beer bottle. "For what?"

"For coming over, for bringing food. For just being a friend when I needed one."

"Eh." He shrugs. "It helps that you've got a big dick."

I grab a throw pillow from underneath me and hit him in the face with it. "Just shut up and tell me how the week at work was."

21

———

GAEL

IT FELT SO weird being home, and I couldn't work out why. My house was the same, and I remembered living here with Elena, our life together, and the simple things like where everything was located. But I still felt a disconnect I couldn't explain.

It didn't help that the harder I tried to ignore the change within me, the more noticeable it felt. And not just to me.

It had been almost a week, and I had lashed out at Elena no less than a dozen times. I felt like an absolute prick, but I couldn't stop myself.

She would hover or ask questions or worry, and it all grated on my nerves in a way that was unwarranted and unexplainable.

My parents and sisters had worked out a rotating schedule between them to come over and check on me when they were "in the area." Or to secretly keep an eye on me when Elena needed to leave.

I knew it was something they had all discussed behind my back, and the need to be alone heightened with every "random" visit.

The only person who hadn't come to see me since helping Elena get me settled in at home was Jordan, and I was fucking livid about it. He'd texted and called to tell me catching up on work after Vegas was keeping him busy, and because of that, I hadn't seen him in the flesh and it made me feel like a madman.

He was the only one I wanted to see. Only one I wanted to talk to.

I knew how unfair that was to everyone else who had dropped their entire lives for me, but he had always known what to do and how to handle me. And how to put me in my place when I needed it. This situation shouldn't have been any different. But it was. Because to put me in my place, he'd need to *be* here. And he wasn't, and I hated it because I didn't know why.

When I wasn't asleep, I was trying to work out how this retrograde amnesia worked. My memory regarding the trip was completely non-existent, and I seemed to have trouble searching through anything immediately before that. But when Elena or any one of my family members mentioned things from the past, even as recent as Christmas, my mind had no problem following along and remembering. I just couldn't seem to pinpoint every memory myself.

And since Jordan was missing in action, I asked Elena to walk me through everything that led to Vegas. Even though her version was limited, she started at the Christmas gift exchange, which I remembered, including Seth and Ray joining us. I had no recollection of Julian and Deacon meeting us in Vegas or the fact that we had all rung in the new year together.

The new year had also meant that I was supposed to be back from winter break and teaching at Greensday. But that was on hold indefinitely.

I had tests to pass and things to prove before anyone allowed me to do anything, including be back in my class-room, and for some reason this meant Elena thought she needed to stay home with me too.

"You've already had two whole weeks off," I remind her as I lay down in my bed with my eyes closed. "I don't think you need to miss another one. Your students are likely to riot."

"I have vacation time," she argues, her voice traveling around the room as she puts away laundry. "And I'm not comfortable being away from you yet."

I open my eyes as I feel a dip in the mattress. Elena climbs up onto the bed and nestles beneath the blankets. With her body beside mine, she throws her arm around my chest. I pull her close to me. "What's wrong?"

"Nothing," she murmurs.

"Elena."

She lets out a heavy sigh. "I just can't seem to get that image of you lying there on the hospital bed out of my mind." I can feel her tears land on my shirt. "So, I don't want to rush your recovery or rush my time at home with you."

And this was exactly what I was struggling to come to terms with. I knew everyone had suffered. I knew everyone was relieved that I was alive and okay and somewhat on the mend.

But besides being grateful I was alive, I didn't share any of the same sentiments. I was stuck somewhere between "I can't explain how I'm feeling" and "nobody understands anyway."

And lying here with Elena was the perfect example, because I empathized, and I appreciated her taking care of me, but I just didn't feel the same relief that she did. I didn't share the need to wrap myself around her and never let go. I wasn't overcome with love or emotion.

I was the most indifferent I'd ever been about anything in my life, and I hated it.

With my arm still around her, I drop a kiss on the top of her head, because the action alone will hopefully make her feel more understood and valued than my words ever could.

"Let's go to sleep," I suggest. The perfect way to run away from something without really moving. "Everything always looks better in the morning."

I don't know who the words are supposed to comfort more, her or me, but I put them out there hoping for exactly that.

Desperately wishing that with a brand-new day I felt more like the man she loved and the man who loved her back.

More like *me* and less like *this*.

"SHE LOOKS BEAUTIFUL, DOESN'T SHE?" I don't recognize the voice, but I raise my head just in time to catch Elena walking through the church doors, my sisters on either side of her. She's wearing a V-necked, ivory satin dress that flares out at the waist, holding a gorgeous bouquet of yellow roses. She looks prettier than any bride that's ever come before her.

Light brown wavy hair frames her face, her smile blinding and beautiful as she walks toward me.

When she reaches me at the front of the altar, I hold my hand out to her, and she places her palm against mine. But instead of looking at me, her attention has shifted to some-thing else. Someone else.

I follow her gaze as her smile fades, my eyes landing on a grief-stricken Jordan.

Standing beside me as my best man, he's all buttoned up in a well fitted tuxedo, but tears just keep silently falling down his face.

"What's wrong?" I ask, dropping Elena's hand and turning to face him.

The words leave my mouth, but there's no sound. He can't hear me.

"Jordan," I say more forcefully. "Why are you crying? What's wrong?"

My voice still doesn't reach him, the questions still unanswered. Stepping forward, I place my hands on either side of his face.

"Jordan," I coax. "Jordan, talk to me."

My thumbs swipe at his cheeks, trying to rid him of the tears, but they just keep coming. His eyes are an ocean of pain, and I can't work out how to get rid of it. "Please talk to me," I beg. "Tell me what's wrong."

The anguish inside my chest begins to morph into panic. I finally manage to tear my eyes away from his, needing help, wanting to know if anyone can figure out why he's so heartbroken.

But there's nobody around us anymore and we're no longer in the church.

When I look back at him the tears have stopped. His eyes are still wet, but now he's smiling.

Confusion has my eyes darting all around, trying to figure out my surroundings, trying to understand the sudden change, but I can't put the puzzle pieces together.

"Jordan." My hands drop from his face, my voice is shaky and confused. "What's happening? Why were you crying? Are you okay?"

He doesn't answer a single question. This time he just walks away, and it's then I realize we're back in the church and he's leaving the same way Elena came in.

"Jordan," I call out, my feet stuck to the ground. "Where are you going?"

He stops to glance over his shoulder. "Well, are you coming or not?"

CONTRARY TO POPULAR BELIEF, sleep did not make everything look better in the morning. Fragmented parts of the dream I had lingered in my subconscious, gnawing at me. I was anxious and confused, trying to make sense of it and then inexplicably crabby because I couldn't.

I couldn't watch TV, I couldn't read, I couldn't concentrate on anything for too long without my head hurting. And not being able to use my right arm just added insult to injury.

I'm lying on the couch when Elena asks, "Are you still up for Deacon and Julian to come over this afternoon?"

The urge to say no is almost instant, but I had already canceled on them once before. And when I open my eyes and see her standing in the kitchen putting together a grazing platter of sorts, the selfish request dies on my tongue.

"Yes," I reply. "I might have to have a nap beforehand, but it will be good to see them."

———

"I'M sorry Deacon couldn't make it," Julian says. "He had some last-minute emergency at the garage with Wade."

"On the weekend?" Elena asks, placing the platter from earlier on the coffee table as we take a seat on our couches.

"They were closed for Christmas and New Year's so it's been a mad rush since they opened back up," he explains.

"And how's work?"

"Well." He pulls a long, slim wrapped up box out of the inside of his jacket, along with a card. "This is a get well soon gift from everyone."

"How did you even fit that in there?" I ask rhetorically, taking the gift from him. I stick the box in between my body and cast and start to awkwardly rip off the paper.

"I can help with that," Elena says. I glance up at her and whatever look is on my face has her rising up off the couch and heading to the front door. She grabs her coat off the hook and threads her arms through.

"Where are you going?" I ask, my eyes darting between her and Julian, who looks like he'd rather be anywhere but here.

"I'm going for a walk. I'll be back." She shrugs and gives Julian an apologetic look before darting her gaze back to mine. "I've got my phone if you need anything."

The apartment rattles as she slams the door behind her, and I angrily toss the half-opened gift onto the couch beside me. "Fuck," I shout.

Julian leans over and picks up the gift. He finishes unwrapping it and then opens the box to reveal a Da Vinci oil paintbrush, with my name engraved in the wood.

It's beautiful and expensive, and I feel like the biggest piece of shit for running Elena out of her own house.

Shame and anger heat my skin as I meet Julian's eyes and take the box out of his hand and place it on the table.

"Want to tell me what that was about?" he asks casually.

"I'm a fucking mess," I confess, running my hand

through my hair. "I know I've only been home for a week, but I am a *fucking* mess."

I point to the door. "I snap at her every day, multiple times a day, and I don't know why and I don't know how to make it stop."

"It's a lot being in one another's space all the time, and you have a serious head injury. Give yourself some time to adjust."

"And what, be a dick to her in the meantime?"

He sighs. "Gael, I didn't say that."

Resigned, I let my body sag into the couch. "I'm not the same," I tell him. "And the whole not remembering thing, it's driving me insane."

"Jordan said something to me about you not remembering the trip. Didn't even remember Deacon and me being there."

I shake my head at him. "Not a single thing. And it shouldn't matter. But I feel like my equilibrium is off."

He smirks. "I think that's the head injury."

"Shut up," I groan, a smile tugging at my lips.

"But seriously, why don't you just ask Jordan to fill you in?"

My scowl returns at the mention of his name, and *that* had never happened before. I had never felt this hurt and angry, and I didn't even have a reason to feel this way toward him. He didn't owe me his time, but every part of me, irrational or not, wanted him here, and I couldn't work out why he didn't want to be with me. "He'd have to do more than text me to be able to fill me in."

Julian tilts his head in confusion. "Come again?"

"I think he's avoiding me. And I can't work out why."

Julian scrubs a hand over his face. "You should talk to him."

"Do you know something I don't?" I laugh humorlessly as my own words hit my ears. "Oh, wait, everybody knows something I don't."

"Just talk to him," he implores. "He's your best friend, he's not going anywhere. And we both know how he feels about you."

Trust Julian to be the one to bring up Jordan's feelings about me; he did it often. The feelings we never speak of and pretend they don't exist.

"Something's different with him since the accident, though."

"He could still be a little thrown off by witnessing the crash. It's a hard image to get out of your head."

And once again, I remind myself just how lucky I am to have gotten out safely and alive.

"I know if I watched that happen to Deacon"—he swallows hard, getting emotional at just the thought—"to be so close to losing him like that? I would never be the same either."

I got it. I did. I got the fear and the worry and the unease. But I'm here and I'm okay, and I still felt like I was the one who was close to losing *him*.

22

JORDAN

I STARED at the text on my screen.

Elena: Why haven't you come over? Gael's waiting for you.

It was both unexpected and warranted.

I was hiding from my best friend when he needed me the most, and if Elena was calling me out on it, then it was clear my absence had been noticed.

It's not like I didn't want to see him, because I did. I miss him and wanted to spend all my spare time with him, but I had only been to Gael's apartment a handful of times since Elena moved in. I had always felt like the third wheel as I watched them turn his place into their home.

And I didn't expect now to be any different. In fact, I expected it to be worse, because if Elena felt even half of what I felt about Gael, she wouldn't let him out of her sight.

The hospital had been our own little bubble. Taking each day one at a time and co-existing for the greater good. I'd pushed everything I felt for him to the back of my mind, for as long as I could, but now Elena was living the life that had slipped between my fingertips, and I couldn't reconcile how to stay away from her without staying away from him.

I was being torn in half doing right by their relationship and doing right by me. And it was hurting us both.

I text Elena back.

Me: I've just been giving you two some time and space.

Elena: He doesn't want space.

The three dots bounce repeatedly on the screen for a ridiculously long time. When the message comes through, I know why.

Elena: He just wants you.

I don't have the chance to respond when another text comes through.

Elena: He has a doctor's appointment at 1. Take him. Please.

I felt like I was living in the Twilight Zone, or like I was walking into a trap.

This wasn't her. This wasn't how our relationship was, but then again, neither one of us were the same anymore.

And she was right, he didn't want space. We'd never given one another space in our whole entire lives. I shouldn't have made this any different.

Me: I'll pick him up and take him.

Elena: Thank you.

There's a knock on my office door and Frankie walks in without waiting for me to invite him in.

"Why do you even bother knocking?" I ask.

He ignores me, putting a coffee on my desk. "Why do you look like that?"

"Like what?"

"Like you've seen a ghost."

I hand him my cell, open to the text exchange.

"What are you doing here then?" he questions, his tone more annoyed than curious.

"The text said the appointment was at one, it's only nine-thirty."

"For fuck's sake, Jordan, he's your best friend. You don't need scheduled time with your best friend." He slides the phone across my desk. "He needs you. You found each other once. You can't make it happen again if you don't see him."

Frankie turns to walk out of the office when I call him back. He glances at me over his shoulder. "What?"

"Do you really believe that?"

He nods. "For you, I do."

Moving on impulse, I grab the coffee, my keys, my cell, and my coat off the rack on my way out the door.

My office is only a twenty-minute drive to Gael's apartment, and with a stop for some donuts and coffee, I'm there knocking on his door in half an hour.

When Gael answers the door and his face drops, I know just how much I've hurt him with my absence.

"I'm sorry." I extend my arm out, offering the coffee and donuts as an apology.

He grabs them with his uninjured hand and walks away from me. If we were an actual couple this would be comical.

"Gael," I call out.

I follow him inside the apartment, closing the door behind me. "Where's Elena?" I ask.

"She's back at work."

"Already?"

He whirls around like a tornado. "What's she supposed to do, just stay home and wait on me hand and foot?"

"Hey." I put my hands up in surrender. "I should've clarified. I didn't think *she'd* want to go back so soon."

He places my peace offering on the counter and then turns to face me, looking extremely unimpressed.

"What are you doing here?" he spits out, but the question he really wanted to ask is written all over his scowling face. *Where have you been?*

This was a new version of him. A side I'd never seen. He was angry and impatient, and in a different world, I would be so turned on by the way his desperation for me changed him.

But that had no place here, because he was struggling and I wasn't helping. Not like I promised I would, not like the best friend he'd grown up with should.

Closing the gap between us, I walk toward him. "Tell me how to make it better."

He shakes his head, surprising me when unshed tears fill his eyes. "If I knew, do you think I'd be feeling like this?"

I had never seen him look any more broken, or any more distraught than I did right now, and all I wanted was to scoop him up in my arms, promise it would get better, and never let him go.

"Come here," I say, emotion thick in my voice. Grabbing his wrist, I tug him to me. He throws one arm around my neck and I work around his broken arm and hold him to me.

It was dangerous being this close to him, feeling his body flush with mine. And if Gael thought the way we were holding each other was different or weird or unlike us, he didn't say a single word.

Instead, I just told myself to focus on what Frankie had said, about how maybe we could find one another again.

I just had to remind him what he was looking for.

We stand there in silence for a decent stretch, his heart beating in time with mine. I don't rush him or probe him for answers or even ask him a million questions he seems to be struggling to answer.

I just wait. Wait for him to find his own words, to come to terms with whatever this is in his own way.

"What are you doing here?" he asks again, the hostility missing this time.

"I was overdue for a visit," I offer, deliberately being vague. "Maybe we can just hang out together before your doctor's appointment."

He pulls his head back to get a better look at me. "How do you know about my doctor's appointment?"

"Elena told me," I admit.

I feel his body rise as he takes a long, deep breath, only for him to step away from me and lean on the counter as he exhales. "I'm not used to this," he says.

"To what?"

"All the fussing and the hovering and the micro-managing."

"You mean the caring?" I say with a hint of sarcasm.

He rolls his eyes. "I know everyone means well, but I'm at my wits' end, Jordan. I'm not used to everyone doing things for me and worrying and obsessing." He points at his chest. "That's my job. It's always been my job, and I like it that way."

Hearing him talk about himself, referring to the man he's always been, and recognizing it, remembering it, has a flutter of hope shimmying through my chest.

"Every now and then the caretaker needs to be taken care of."

"I don't like it."

I can't help but laugh. "You don't have to. It doesn't mean the people who love you aren't going to gladly do for you what you're always doing for them."

I watch the Adam's apple in his throat bob. "Maybe."

I don't argue with him, because history told me there was no point when he was like this. Instead, I reach for his coffee and hand it to him and then open the box of donuts.

"Are you worried about your appointment today?" Even though I had physically stayed away, Gael and I had texted often. I had called to check in just as much, but I knew Gael would avoid talking about the side effects of the accident if he could. "Did they give you any indication of what to expect?"

"It's just a follow up," he says. "I really want to get cleared for work and driving, but I don't see that happening just yet."

"How do you know that?"

"They're going to ask me if the headaches have gone or how my concentration is and if my eyes hurt," he says. "And the answers to those questions aren't getting my life back to normal any quicker."

"Answer those questions for me." I can tell he doesn't want to but I insist. "And I want the truth."

"They're all improving," he says. "The headaches, my vision, my concentration, they're all getting better, hurting less, happening less, but they're not gone, and I can't do anything until they are."

"Are you painting or drawing?"

He stiffens when I ask him and it's clear I've struck a nerve. "Well, are you?"

"I have been," he supplies. "But don't ask me to show anything to you because the answer is no."

So touchy.

"Same old. Same old," I quip lightly, remembering how he only ever showed you the finished product of something he'd been working on.

"But what about you?" He changes the subject smoothly. "What's been happening at work that's kept you so busy?"

It's the smallest hint of a call out. A little bit of accusation with a sliver of curiosity.

"Frankie finally landed that huge apartment complex contract he'd been working on. That's a huge win for the company."

I don't miss the way his jaw clenches at the mention of Frankie, and I can't help but joke. "I guess the accident didn't change the way you feel about him."

He glares at me. "Are you still going to bring him home to meet the family?"

He says it so casually that I don't bring attention to how easily the reference to something before the accident rolled off his tongue.

"Nah," I say nonchalantly. "He's not the one for me."

———

THE MORNING FLIES BY, Gael and I falling into an easy, familiar rhythm. Talking and joking and laughing.

And if you didn't look hard enough, it was easy to think absolutely nothing had changed. But I knew him well. I had spent my whole adult life memorizing everything about him and I didn't miss how the light didn't reach his eyes anymore.

He was trying. He was trying so goddamn hard, it hurt to watch, but his spark was missing. He was a little lost and confused, and not just about the obvious things. It was also the things he couldn't see and touch and understand that were throwing him off balance.

A little part of me wanted to believe he missed me and what we'd become in those days before the accident. That he felt the loss just as much as I did.

The doctor's door swings open and Gael steps outside. I'd hoped to see a sliver of excitement upon his return, but a disheartened look on his face told me the appointment didn't go to plan.

Rising to my feet, I stand beside him as he schedules another appointment in two weeks' time.

When we're walking back to my car, I break the silence.

"What did he say?"

"I'm probably never going to remember those days in Vegas," he blurts out.

"That's not what I was expecting you to say."

He tilts his head to look at me. "What do you mean?"

"I thought you went to see how long it would be till you could go back to work or get behind a wheel."

"I did. But I also asked about the memories, and he said it might just be a time in my life I wouldn't remember."

"That doesn't seem like the answer you were looking for."

"It's not," he says angrily.

"You know your recovery isn't dependent on the memories, right?"

"I know, but I still don't like not knowing."

Sticking my hand in my pocket, I find the key fob to my car and start it. We both climb in, and as the blanket of warmth from my heater settles over us, I reach over and put my hand on his thigh but make sure his honey brown eyes are only looking at me.

"Gael," I say gently. "There was nothing to it." The lie tastes like acid on my tongue. "It was a guys' trip away. Drinking, eating, and gambling. Rinse and repeat."

His leg bounces furiously underneath my palm. He tears his gaze away from mine, looking out the window. "Yeah, okay," he mutters.

Guilt swelled in my chest. This was the biggest secret I had ever kept from him, and it was making me feel ill. Bile burned my throat, stopping any words of comfort from slipping out of my mouth. Because they weren't just words anymore, they were blatant lies.

So much more had happened in Vegas, and it was hovering over us like a big, black storm cloud just waiting to ruin us with its downpour.

Ten minutes into the drive, Gael's phone rings. He stares at the screen, Elena's contact photo right there staring back at him. "Are you going to answer?"

Wordlessly, he swipes at the screen and brings it up to his ear. "Hello."

Reminiscent of that morning in Vegas, I listen to a one-sided conversation between Gael and Elena. But this time, I know we're on the same wavelength. I can imagine what she's saying, and I can imagine the depth of her concern, and not for the first time in all of this, I know the love she has for Gael means that we're constantly worried for him.

Since Gael avoided telling me everything that happened with his neurologist, I eavesdrop on the conversation and am grateful to hear that his progress is on track. Albeit not as fast as he would like it, but he's moving forward. And that's enough for me.

When he hangs up, he glances over at me. "I don't want to go back home yet."

"Anywhere in particular you want to go?"

He shakes his head, and my heart stumbles over a beat as he smiles for what feels like the first time since the accident. "You know I'd go anywhere with you."

23

GAEL

"SHE LOOKS BEAUTIFUL, DOESN'T SHE?" I don't recognize the voice, but I raise my head just in time to catch Elena walking through the church doors, my sisters on either side of her. She's wearing a V-necked, ivory satin dress that flares out at the waist, holding a gorgeous bouquet of yellow roses. She looks prettier than any bride that's ever come before her.

Light brown wavy hair frames her face, her smile blinding and beautiful as she walks toward me.

When she reaches me at the front of the altar, I hold my hand out to her, and she places her palm against mine. But instead of looking at me, her attention has shifted to something else. Someone else.

I follow her gaze as her smile fades, my eyes landing on a grief-stricken Jordan.

Standing beside me as my best man, he's all buttoned up in a well fitted tuxedo, but tears just keep silently falling down his face.

"What's wrong?" I ask, dropping Elena's hand and turning to face him.

The words leave my mouth, but there's no sound. He can't hear me.

"Jordan," I say more forcefully. "Why are you crying? What's wrong?"

My voice still doesn't reach him, the questions still unanswered. Stepping forward, I place my hands on either side of his face.

"Jordan," I coax. "Jordan, talk to me."

My thumbs swipe at his cheeks, trying to rid him of the tears, but they just keep coming. His eyes are an ocean of pain, and I can't work out how to get rid of it. "Please talk to me," I beg. "Tell me what's wrong."

The anguish inside my chest begins to morph into panic. I finally manage to tear my eyes away from his, needing help, wanting to know if anyone can figure out why he's so heartbroken.

But there's nobody around us anymore and we're no longer in the church.

When I look back at him, the tears have stopped. His eyes are still wet, but now he's smiling.

Confusion has my eyes darting all around, trying to figure out my surroundings, trying to understand the sudden change, but I can't put the puzzle pieces together.

"Jordan." My hands drop from his face, my voice is shaky and confused. "What's happening? Why were you crying? Are you okay?"

He doesn't answer a single question. This time he just walks away, and it's then I realize we're back in the church and he's leaving the same way Elena came in.

"Jordan," I call out, my feet stuck to the ground. "Where are you going?"

He stops to glance over his shoulder. "Well, are you coming or not?"

. . .

I WAS LYING down on the couch at my parents' house, needing to close my eyes. My nieces and nephews were noisily tiptoeing around me, trying to be quiet.

The irony wasn't lost on me, but I loved them for it.

Since the accident, everyone had been sporadically spending time at my apartment instead of gathering for weekly dinner at my parents' place, but after the promising news from the doctor and the great afternoon I had with Jordan at the Center on Contemporary Art, I figured I owed it to everyone to lighten up a bit.

Except, as the days after progressed, and I was still home alone while everybody's lives kept moving, I began to fall into that familiar slump that seemingly became harder and harder for me to climb out of.

And like clockwork, every time Elena noticed it becoming a problem, she dragged me out of the house. Today we were finally going to be the ones who visited my parents instead of them making the trip to see us.

I knew she hoped a bit of normalcy and the return of routine—doing all the things we used to do before the setbacks of my accident went and complicated everything— would make everything better, but it was useless. I was broken.

And even more noticeably, *we* were broken.

Nothing was the same between us, and I could desperately see her trying to hold on, while I felt myself continuously slipping away.

I couldn't tell whether the evolution of our relationship had stopped because of the accident or because we were finally realizing that we had spent too much time trying to fix something that would always be broken.

I knew she loved me, and I did love her, but as each day passed, it just didn't feel like the type of love that could weather this storm.

"Hey, Mama Bear." Jordan's voice carries through the house announcing his arrival, and the restlessness inside my chest settles at the simple sound.

"Where have you been, Jordan Varga?" my mom asks. "You have been hiding."

"You just used my full name. I must be in trouble."

"You're all in trouble," she says. "I haven't had my whole family here in weeks."

The back of my eyes sting as I hear the worry in my mother's voice. The silence that lingers has me getting off the couch and walking to the foyer.

My mother has her small arms around Jordan's torso, her head only reaching his sternum. He's bent awkwardly, his face turned in my direction, his cheek resting on the top of her head.

I knew she was crying; she'd cried a lot this last month. But she tried so hard to be everyone else's rock, she forgot to let someone else be hers.

When a tear slips down his face, past his nose and into my mother's hair, an image of him crying at my wedding flashes in my mind.

I'd had the same dream since coming home. Me getting married and him crying. Night after night, he'd ask me if I was coming with him, and I just stood there, stuck to the ground, in limbo.

These tears were different. They were shared tears, tears we had all cried and ones we all understood.

My mom angles her head just enough to see me. "Well, what are you doing just standing there? I need both my boys hugging me."

Not one to not listen to his mother, I stretch my good arm around them, my hand brushing past Jordan's. He grabs it, and I can't think of a single reason not to let him hold it.

"Hey." Three heads turn to the sound of Mariana's voice. "How come we didn't get the call up?"

My eyes land on Elena who's wedged in the doorway, between my sisters, and while they're focused on how "adorable" we all look, Elena's got nothing but heartbreak in her eyes and a hue of embarrassment and anger on her cheeks.

Her gaze darts between Jordan, me, our clasped hands, and back up to Jordan. "Don't move on my account."

They share a look, and for the first time since the accident, I really feel like everybody knows something I don't.

His jaw clenches, and I try to pull my hand away but he holds on tighter.

"Jordan," I say sternly.

Reluctantly, he lets go of my hand, and even though I know in my gut he's keeping something from me, the loss of his skin on mine still hits hard.

I look at both of them, trying to work out what's going on, but they're now staring at me like I'm the one with the answers. Like somehow I can make this all better.

"Fuck this," Elena mutters. She pushes past my sisters, and I'm standing there trying to work up the courage to leave Jordan behind, but I can't.

Because now that Elena's walked out of the room, he's dropped the anger and he's looking at me with a desolation so deep it slices my heart in two.

"What aren't you telling me?" I ask him.

He shakes his head, and his refusal to be honest helps me make the impossible choice.

I step away from him and my mother, ignoring how

much it hurts and all the confused looks from my family, and dart straight for her.

"Elena, wait," I call out. She keeps walking through the house, now heading straight for the bathroom. "Elena."

I manage to reach her in time, sticking my good hand in between the door and the frame. I push against it, locking it behind me once I'm inside.

With her hands on the edge of the basin, she stands there looking in the mirror, trying to regulate her short and shallow breathing. I adjust myself to fit in the small space, sliding in right behind her, our eyes meeting in the reflection.

"What was that about?" I ask in anger, tipping my head back in the direction we all came from. "Between you and Jordan. What am I missing?"

Shaking her head, she wipes at her cheek with the back of her hand. "I don't want to do this here, Gael."

"Well, we can go home," I bite back.

"And take you away from your mom who's been crying all day because she's just so happy you're here?"

"Well, what the fuck is going on right now?" I bellow. "Because I know there's something you're definitely not telling me."

"Stop," she snaps, her tone cutting through weeks of hell she's gone through with me. "Stop." Her second demand loses its anger, as a pained sob slips between her lips. "I said I don't want to do this here."

When I don't move, she drags her distressed gaze off my reflection and turns one of the taps on, waiting for the hot water to come out. "Just get out, Gael," she says, her voice cold and even. "If you want to do something for me, just do *that*."

———

IF ELENA ever wanted to take up a career in acting, she could've won an Oscar for outstanding performance in a family drama, and my family would've taken out all the awards for the supporting roles.

Because they were all sitting here around the dinner table, talking and joking, acting like I wasn't a loose cannon who was vibrating with anger in my seat.

She talked and laughed and ate like she didn't have a care in the world. She occasionally touched my hand, curled an arm around my bicep, leaned her head on my shoulder.

For whatever reason, she would not stop touching me.

And that meant the only person who wouldn't look at me was the one person I wanted desperately to do so. I didn't know what I wanted from him more, the truth or the attention.

As the night progressed, I knew Elena was staking a claim on me, and I felt sick inside every time she did it. And not because she didn't have every right to, but because she was hurting him. On purpose. And I didn't know why.

For whatever reason, he took it in stride. Only speaking when spoken to, keeping his attention to the kids to avoid meeting anyone's gaze.

When his cell rang, he stepped into another room to take the call, and I couldn't help but untangle myself from Elena and follow him.

I caught the tail end of the conversation and waited for him to notice me in the room.

When he turned around and saw me, he startled.

"Everything okay?" he asks.

"No," I say truthfully. "Everything is not okay."

"I don't know what you want me to say," he says. His voice is calm, but his eyes held the truth. They were as turbulent as I felt.

"Gael," Elena's voice cuts through our conversation before I even have the time to respond to him. "I'm not feeling well, do you think we could go?"

I scoff, loud enough for both of them to hear. The irony. *She* wasn't feeling well.

Jordan's gaze remains fixated on the floor, unable to look at me or Elena, and I feel like my heart is at the center of a pendulum swing, and they're taking turns pushing it back and forth between themselves.

Looking at him but talking to her, I say, "I'll be out in a second."

When it's just me and him again, I decide against waiting for him to come to me with the truth.

"Are you free tomorrow?" I ask him.

"For you? Always. You know that."

And that's why I was always so weak for him. His heart is huge. His ability to say all the right things, when you need to hear them most, one of the reasons he's loved by so many.

"I'll meet you at your place first thing in the morning," I tell him.

"Let me pick you up."

"No," I say, adamantly sick of being the broken man everybody needed to chauffeur around. "I can get my own way there."

"Okay," he agrees. "I'll be waiting."

I offer him a parting nod and leave the room to say goodbye to my family. Sensing the tension, each one of them hugs me tightly, kindly choosing not to press or prod, except for my mom.

"*Mijo*, what's going on? Why are you all angry at each other?"

"We're okay," I lie. "Nothing that can't be fixed."

"I don't want you to work yourself up. You're supposed to have a stress-free recovery."

I cradle her petite face in my large hands and kiss both of her cheeks. "I love you, Mama. We'll all be okay."

Grateful that my words can at least reassure one of us, I wave goodbye one more time and head to the car.

We sit in silence as Elena drives us home, either too angry or too exhausted to talk. But when we make it into our apartment, her emotions are all back on alert as she grabs one of my small suitcases and begins packing.

"What are you doing?" I ask her.

"I'm going home for a few days."

I narrow my eyes at her. "This is your home."

"No." She storms into the bedroom and comes back out with a heap of clothes. "This is *your* home. I just live here."

"Elena," I say firmly, but she doesn't even stop to glance at me. When she ignores me for a second time, I invade her personal space and make her look at me. "This is your home."

"It doesn't matter what it is," she says, her chin trembling. "I need some space. Some time to think."

"I can leave," I offer. "I can go to my parents' place or one of my sisters'. You hate it there."

"It's my home, Gael. Whether I like it or not, it's all I have right now."

"Elena—"

"Don't." She puts a hand up between us. "Don't be nice, caring, wonderful Gael right now. I can't handle it. Please."

"We need to talk," I remind her.

"I know," she says, her voice losing a little of the infuriation. "I know. About us and about tonight. I know all of this, but I need a few days."

"Okay." I nod in agreement, knowing after how horrible I've been to her since the accident, I owe her this. "A few days. But you come back if it gets to be too much over there."

She continues to pack, and I watch her in silence, not really sure if there's anything more I can say, or how I really feel.

It only takes her half an hour to wrangle her things together into two small suitcases she wheels to the door.

"Let me take them to the car for you." I bend to pick them up and she covers my hand with hers, stopping me.

"No. I've got this."

Tears well in her eyes, and I hate myself for doing this to her. "I've made you cry a lot lately, haven't I?"

She cups my cheek and runs her thumb across my lips. "But there was a time when you made me smile and laugh a lot too."

24

———

ELENA

IT'S MIDNIGHT, and I feel unhinged as I beat Jordan's door down.

"Jordan," I shout. Bang. Bang. Bang. "Jordan, open up."

I raise my fist, ready to hit the wood, but this time the door swings open, and my whole body falls forward, landing on Jordan's chest.

"Whoa." His arms grip my biceps and he pushes me back, allowing me to straighten my body. His hair is all rumpled and there are sleep lines all over his face. "Elena, what are you doing here? Is something wrong with Gael?"

I swipe at my tear-stained eyes, absently wondering if I would ever stop crying, before I pull out a scrunched-up piece of paper from my pocket and slap it onto his chest.

I push past him, inviting myself inside his house, pacing like a madwoman.

When I don't hear his footsteps behind me, I look over my shoulder and find him with his head down, reading the paper.

"What?" I ask, an ugly laugh bubbling up from my throat. "You have nothing to say?"

"Where did you get this?" He walks toward me slow and steady, as if he's approaching a wild animal. "Elena, this is not what it looks like."

I tear the creased paper out of his hands and begin to read it for what feels like the hundredth time tonight.

"Gael and Jordan's Regrets & Resolutions List," I read aloud. "You know at first, when it came flying out of the suitcase I was using, I thought it was yours. I've known you long enough to know you love these lists. But then I kept on reading."

He winces, and I do my very best to make it as uncomfortable for him as I possibly can.

I clear my throat dramatically. "Number one: Apologize to Elena."

"Elena."

I can hear him say my name, but I continue to talk over him, allowing my voice to get louder. "Number two: Tell our family. Number three: Move in together. Number four —" My voice shakes, losing all the confidence and hostility. "Number four," I cry. I cry for the very thing I've lost and the very thing they'll gain. "Think about starting a family together."

Large arms wrap around me, but I push my way out of his hold. With shaky hands, I raise the paper to his face. "Tell me, Jordan," I seethe. "Tell me how this isn't what it looks like."

"Elena, I can't..." His voice is nothing but pained anguish that I feel down to my soul. "Elena, I don't..."

I cover my face with my hands, trying to calm myself down. "You can't what, Jordan?" I say steadily. "You don't want to what? You can't tell me my fiancé cheated on me, or you don't want to because he doesn't remember doing it?"

"All of it." He throws his hands in the air and screams.

"It wasn't supposed to happen this way. Not for you or him or me. This isn't how it was supposed to happen."

"Are you sure?" I argue. "Because from where I'm standing, no matter which way it happened, I'm still the only one with a broken heart."

"We didn't mean—" He shakes his head. "He didn't mean—"

"Don't defend him," I exclaim. "The man at home, beating himself up over how moody he's been after the accident. About how he's treated me and all the tears I've cried this last month." I point to his front door. "That man doesn't mean to hurt me."

"But the man you were with in Vegas? He knew very well what he was doing. He just didn't care."

Jordan interrupts me. "He loves you, Elena."

"I know." I nod and blow out a shaky breath and look him square in the eye. "But he loves you more."

Losing my bravado, my voice drops a few notes. "Before he left, something in my gut told me he wouldn't come back the same. But I sat in the car and begged him to come back to me. I told him I knew you two had a connection, but I *needed* him to come back to *me*."

A humorless laugh leaves my mouth. "Do you know what I got instead? I got a hollow shell of the man I love, who left his heart in Vegas with yours."

"I love him," Jordan says firmly. "I have always loved him. And despite all that, I was resigned to living a life where he chose you."

"But then he threw us both a curveball and chose you."

"When he woke up and didn't remember, I thought I could go back," he explains. "I thought I could just settle for his friendship, because if he was happy with you once, he could be happy with you again."

"But he's not happy," I admit in defeat. "He's anything but happy."

My legs weaken at the revelation and Jordan catches me. "Here." He guides me to his couch. "Let me get you a bottle of water."

I grab his forearm. "I don't want water."

He glances down at my hand and back up at me, my grip never loosening. "What do you want, Elena?"

The question was loaded, because I wanted so many things. I wanted to scream and cry and hate the world for all the heartache I had endured, but I wasn't going to do that here in Jordan's house.

I'd come here with questions and I'd gotten the answers I needed, but Gael was still living in the dark, and until he knew the truth, none of us could move on.

"You need to tell Gael about Vegas."

25

GAEL

IT WAS seven in the morning and I was standing on my best friend's porch, almost freezing to death, not caring whether or not he'd had a good night's sleep or that I was very much determined to wake him up.

Last night after Elena left, I had gone through a gamut of emotions, hating that the most prevalent one was relief. I was absolutely devastated by the fact that I was hurting her. Intentionally or not, I had pushed her away with my disregard of her needs while I recovered.

I was distant and ungrateful and, just as expected, that wore on her.

And whatever it is that happened at my parents' place didn't help. The look of animosity that Jordan and Elena shared between them was one I couldn't ignore.

It was significant enough for me to know this was more than the usual petty jealousy that I knew existed , but neither of them would explain it and *that* made me uneasy.

Undecided on whether or not to use my key or ring Jordan's doorbell, I wring my fingers together while staring at the front door.

I take a step back when the door swings open and Jordan suddenly appears before me. He crosses his arms over his chest, trying to warm himself up from the cold. "How long are you going to just stand on my porch for?"

"You're awake," I state, surprised. I let my eyes freely roam over him from head to toe, enjoying the calm being in his presence gives me. God, he's just as gorgeous when he's disheveled and tired. "Have you even slept?"

"It's been a long night." He gestures for me to come inside and I do, closing the door behind me. Warmth settles into my cold skin almost immediately as I follow him farther into the house. "I'm guessing by the time, you didn't get much sleep either."

"I haven't gotten a good night's sleep since the accident," I reveal.

He walks straight to the kitchen and beelines to the coffee machine, turning it on. "It's been that bad?"

I shrug. "I wouldn't say bad. It's just not something that comes so easy to me anymore."

I choose not to add how the recurring dream of him crying and me unable to figure out what it means, along with the endless hours I spend ruminating on why I just don't feel like myself anymore are to blame, and instead go for a lighter approach. "It's not like I'm too busy to nap during the day if I need to. People would kill to have my life."

The joke falls flat as Jordan hands me a hot mug of my own and then leans on the counter behind him. "I'm sorry," he says.

"What are you sorry for? It's not your fault I was in a car accident."

"Well,"—he takes a sip of his coffee—"if we're being technical, I did organize the day out at the race track."

I roll my eyes at him while dragging out a stool to sit on. "I don't even have the energy to entertain that idea."

"I didn't say I actually blamed myself for it." He busies himself with something on his kitchen counter, clearly avoiding my gaze.

"Tell me you haven't been sitting here blaming yourself for something that was completely out of your control."

"I haven't," he answers quickly. "I promise I haven't. I just hate that it happened at all."

You and me both.

Jordan and I just stare at each other, an awkward and unexplainable tension brewing between us. We've been friends for longer than we haven't, and never in all those years did it ever feel this unsettled.

It felt like day by day, little by little, I was losing one more thing to the accident.

My ability to drive to work. My perfect health. I'd lost my memory. Last night it was Elena, and now I was trying to work out if today it would be Jordan.

"Are you okay?" Jordan asks me. They're the exact same words he'd said to me yesterday at my mother's house. He isn't the first person to ask the question. Anybody who cares has.

But it hit differently when he asked, because he was the only one I wanted to break down to and tell.

I wasn't okay. In general, everybody knew that, but what I wanted to know was "does it matter?" I blurt it out unintentionally. When his eyebrows narrow in confusion, I clarify. "If I'm not okay, does it even matter?"

He flinches, placing the mug of coffee down on the counter. "What do you mean does it matter? Of course it matters."

"What if..." I pause, trying to find the right words.

"What if it can't be fixed? Does it still matter if it can't be fixed? If *I* can't be fixed."

"Gael." Jordan's pained eyes find mine, unspoken worry and fear and always love shining in them. The love he didn't know I saw, the love I hated him hiding. "There's nothing wrong with you. There's nothing to be fixed."

I shake my head, because it isn't true. There was something wrong. It was like someone had thrown me to the ground and, like glass, I shattered, but they couldn't find all the pieces to put me back together. I had never felt so mismatched in my life. And even though logic told me I had sustained a traumatic brain injury and this was to be expected, I couldn't fathom it.

I couldn't make sense of the change, or maybe I just didn't like the new me.

I was just a walking, talking, empty cavity. And it was the little things too. I was wearing a mask that looked and acted like me but wasn't.

I didn't smile. I didn't joke. I didn't laugh. Not like before. Not with any emotion that felt real.

I might not have remembered the specifics of what happened in Vegas, but I knew with my whole being, that when I was there I didn't feel so lost. And I definitely didn't feel this lonely.

Swept up in my own thoughts, I don't even notice that Jordan has moved closer. He's bent at the waist, his elbows resting on the counter, his hands steepled in front of his mouth.

For the first time, I didn't want his undivided attention. I didn't want to rip myself apart for him to be told it was all in my head.

As if he can read my mind, or maybe every single thought was written on my face, he reaches for both my hands, one of his over the top of mine, the other over the top of my cast.

I looked down, hating that I couldn't feel his skin on mine. When I found the courage to raise my head and meet his gaze, I knew what was coming, what he was waiting for. "Talk to me, Gael."

It didn't matter that I was still so confused about last night and the possibility of a secret between him and Elena, because his concern for me was like a warm, soft blanket and I so desperately wanted to wrap myself in it.

"I don't know how to explain it," I admit. "Not in a way that'll make sense."

"Try me."

"Something doesn't feel right," I say. "And I know about the mood swings, the short temper, and the mental exhaustion that relate to my brain, but…" I slide my hand out of his and place it over my chest. "Something doesn't feel right in *here*."

"What else?" he says softly.

"I feel empty," I admit. "And I feel numb. So numb to things I know I should feel something for." Shame fills me as I continue. "Like Elena. I remember loving her and wanting to marry her, but I can't work out why I don't feel like that now."

"Have you spoken to her?" he asks.

"She went back to her place last night."

"For good?"

"She said she needed a few days." I blow out a tired breath. "I think maybe she hit her quota of days she could sustain being someone's verbal punching bag," I say sarcastically. "But I don't know where we go from here. I don't even know how to go back."

He leans closer and, on instinct, I do too, my eyes

darting to the slow bob in the column of his throat. "And what do you want?"

My gaze finds his.

"I want to know why my heart feels so damn heavy." The emotion that pours out of me as I breathe air into something that makes absolutely no sense can't be contained. "I want to know why I'm sad, and why it feels like I'm grieving, when I don't even know what I've lost."

"Gael."

I shake my head, cutting Jordan off, needing to get all of this out. Because if I don't, it will consume me. It will bury me alive, and I need to know if I'm going fucking crazy.

Feeling anxious and fidgety, I stand up off the stool and pace as I try to gather my thoughts. Stopping, I look at Jordan and point to myself. "I want to know why I feel like there's a gaping hole inside my chest that can't be filled."

It isn't till he walks around the kitchen island and over to me that I realize I've been pacing again.

"Gael," he says calmly, but I'm too worked up to listen.

"I go to sleep and wake up every day with this feeling and it follows me around, all day. It's a dull ache." Jordan stops me, gripping my upper arms, his eyes brimming with heat and hurt and that goddamn heart of his that he's always been too scared to give me.

"It's got its own fucking pulse," I choke out. "Throbbing. Pounding." I put my hand over his heart, mimicking a heartbeat. "Just. Like. That."

My heavy, labored breaths fill the air around us, my voice tired. "Why do I feel like a few days changed my whole fucking life?"

"Gael." His voice is a sad whisper now. His hands glide up over my shoulders, settling on either side of my neck.

"And why does it only all feel better when I'm around you?"

26

JORDAN

IF I WAS SUPPOSED to wait to kiss him, I couldn't.

He was slicing himself open for me. So raw and so vulnerable, and I couldn't make him wait and process all the hard stuff without letting him know that there was nothing wrong with him.

He wasn't lost, or empty, or numb.

He was just heartbroken.

My mouth descends onto his, and I feel his tension disperse beneath my palms. Hands curl around either side of my hips, one firm, and the other awkward and clumsy. Our mouths move against one another in a perfectly synchronized dance.

For a moment, the world is ours.

Gael doesn't push me away or question me, he gladly submits, letting my lips lead him home.

The heat between us is a delicious simmer as our tongues take their time becoming reacquainted.

There's no rush, no panic, no fear. There's no hesitation or hurt. No car accident and no memory loss.

I wasn't stupid enough to think that this would be it.

That this would be what fixed us or immediately made him feel better. I knew we had a long road ahead, but the permanency I felt in this kiss made it better than all the times before.

After a lifetime of loving this man, it was finally going to be Gael and me, right where we were supposed to be.

"We've done this before," he murmurs against my lips, a statement more than a question. "Why didn't you tell me?"

I open my eyes to meet his, my heart rattling at hearing the hurt in his voice. "I didn't know how."

He steps back, away from me, scrubbing his hand over his face. "For weeks, Jordan... for weeks, I've felt like this and you didn't say a single word."

Shaking my head, I lick my lips before speaking. "That's not fair."

"No." His voice rises. "What's not fair is waking up from an accident and finding out you lost your memory."

"You had a fiancée, Gael." I raise my hand up. "You *still* have a fiancée. And I wasn't going to be the one to put you on blast like that. Say, 'hey, just so you know, Gael cheated on you. He's with me now.'"

He slaps at his chest. "But you could've told me!"

"I was scared," I blurt out. "I was so fucking scared."

Stalking toward him, I decide to try a different approach, one that doesn't lead him into a complete panic attack. I wait till the back of his knees hit the couch and he's got nowhere else to go, forcing him to sit down. I manage to angle my large frame, straddling him and purposefully getting all up in his space.

I place my hands on either side of his face, forcing him to look at me, forcing him to listen to me the way he made me listen to him in Vegas. "When we were in Vegas I told you that I wouldn't survive having you and then losing you.

And then I actually almost lost you, and everything changed."

"I was so unprepared," I state. "One minute you were mine and the next? I had to give you up."

The shades of anger in his eyes dull to a hue of hurt as I keep talking. "When Elena stepped into the hospital you were no longer mine."

I loosen my hold on his cheeks, letting my hands fall to his shoulders. "I didn't have a claim on you when she got there. You were mine in the dark and hers in the light. I had to give you back."

His hand fists the front of my t-shirt and he drags me down, my forehead now pressed against his.

"I don't know if I'm mad at you or just mad."

"I don't care which one it is," I say. "Be both. Take however long you need, but just promise to do it while we're together, because I can't stand the thought of being away from you for one more day."

"There's so much I don't know," he says quietly. "What if I never remember?"

"You didn't forget," I say to him. "Your heart and your soul, they never forgot. They never forgot me. Or us."

His eyes light up. "Oh my God."

"What is it?"

"I can't believe I didn't figure it out before."

Struggling to follow along, I patiently wait for him to explain himself.

"I've been having this dream since I got back to Seattle."

"Yeah?"

"It's a dream where I'm supposed to be marrying Elena but you're always crying."

I watch his face fall as he registers the heavy feel of her name on his tongue, remembering that he has a whole other life that he has to deal with before we can figure out if there is one for us.

"Does she know?" he asks me.

Steadily, I climb off him and walk to my bedroom without a word. When I return, I hold the list close to my chest, wanting to give him context before I tell him about what happened last night. "At first, I thought she had an inkling. A few things she said and did, here and there, pointed in that direction."

"Like last night at Mom and Dad's?"

Nodding, I hand him the paper.

"What's this?" he asks, plucking it out of my fingers.

I watch his face as his eyes scan the content, taking in the words, processing just how serious we were about this.

He snaps his head up. "Did we write this up in Vegas?"

"Yeah, but that's not why I'm showing you."

He tilts his head to the side. "I don't understand."

"Elena came over last night," I explain. "To bring me that."

Both our eyes dart to our list of regrets and resolutions. "She's seen it?"

"She has. She mentioned finding it in a suitcase last night, but I didn't put two and two together until you showed up this morning saying she'd left."

"She must have taken the bag I took to Vegas," he clarifies.

"And I must've packed it in there by accident."

He leans forward and rests his elbows on his knees, burying his head in his hands. "I really need to talk to her. I don't even know what to say to her."

Crouching down in front of him, I pull his hands away from his face, making him look at me. I keep my eyes on his as I bring his fingers to my lips, kissing them, wanting, even for a split second, to take away all the pain and the pressure.

"Tell her the truth," I advise. "You two have always had that. Sit her down and tell her exactly what you told me. Tell her how you feel."

I point to his heart. "Just tell her what's in there."

27

———

GAEL

AFTER TEXTING Elena to ask her to meet me, I left Jordan's house to go home and work out what I was going to say to her and what we were going to do next.

No matter how instantaneous the relief was from talking to Jordan and slowly finding out bits and pieces of the truth about us, I couldn't take another step forward with him without talking to Elena first.

As I trudge up the stairs, completely exhausted, both emotionally and physically, I'm surprised to see the apartment door open and boxes piled out front. When I see Elena walking out carrying another one, I quicken my pace and jog up the stairs.

"What are you doing?"

She places the box down and lets out a long exhale as she straightens her back. Her eyes and nose are red and puffy, her lips cracked and peeling. She looks exactly the same way she did when I woke up in the hospital in Vegas. "I'm moving out."

I place a hand on the stack of boxes. "I didn't ask you to do that."

"What am I going to do, Gael? Stay here while you and Jordan play happy family?"

I wince, and her eyes soften. "I'm sorry. I shouldn't have just blurted that out, that was mean and uncalled for. I don't even know if you've spoken to him about it yet."

"Not mean, and not uncalled for." I soften my voice, as if the truth will hurt any less if I deliver it differently. "And yeah, we spoke this morning."

"So you know?" she queries.

"I know I don't want to do this in the stairwell," I tell her.

Following her inside, I close the door behind me and attempt to walk closer to her, but she raises a hand to stop me. "I don't need you to come any closer."

Respecting her wishes, I stay on my side of the room, where we both stare at each other. Her body language has her coming across like a force to be reckoned with, but her glassy, tired eyes give away just how much I hurt her.

"I'm sorry, Elena." She tucks her bottom lip between her teeth to stop herself from crying. "I'm so fucking sorry. I'm sorry for—"

"Stop." Straightening her spine, she shakes her head. "I don't need a laundry list of all the things you're sorry about. I don't want to listen as you try to clear your conscience. That's not what I'm here for."

Her bravado slips and she lets out a sigh. "Nothing justifies you cheating on me, Gael. Absolutely nothing. But I'd be lying to myself if I said I wasn't surprised it happened."

"What do you mean?"

"You were still in love with him while you loved me," she exclaims. "And I was too broken and needy to stop us from happening."

She was right, there was a point in time where I had loved them both. I'm not sure I was ever *in love* with Elena, but when my dreams of a future with Jordan became less of a reality, it pushed me further and further into her arms.

"We were happy," I say to her. "There was a good chunk of time where what we had was real and we were happy. I need you to know that."

She nods in understanding.

"And..." I swallow the hurt and the pain and the loss that I know she felt because of me. "It may have never worked out in the end, but I don't regret asking you to marry me. And I'll never forget that the first time I ever considered becoming someone's father was with you."

The sound of her strangled sob has me rushing to her and hugging her as tightly as I could with one functioning arm. I held her close, because I knew that cry wasn't for me or about me. That cry was for everything we'd lost.

"I'm sorry," I whisper into her ear. "I'm so, so sorry."

She cries into my shoulder, and I have no desire to rush her, to encourage her to be calm or to stop crying. Eventually she pulls back, a small, throaty chuckle leaving her mouth. "This wasn't how this was supposed to go. I wasn't supposed to be this weak, crumbling mess."

"Hey." I take her chin in between my thumb and forefinger and make her look at me. "There has never been anything weak about you, okay? We're all a little broken and we're all a little messy. But you are not weak."

She swats my hand away, tears streaming down her face. "Stop it. I want to keep hating you."

This makes me laugh. "Hate me for as long as you need to."

I look around the room at the boxes she still has to move.

"You know you can stay here and I can move," I say. "I know you dislike living with your sisters."

"Gael, it's fine. Truly. It needs to be done."

"Will you at least let me help you move?"

She looks around the room, possibly sizing up how many more boxes she has to lug down the stairs. "I guess you can carry the light stuff."

Surprisingly, we move in a comfortable silence. Up and down the stairs, making the never-ending boxes fit into every spare space in her car.

Wanting to put a box on the passenger seat, I open the door and see the wedding planner my sisters gave Elena when we got engaged and a framed photo of the two of us with my whole family.

Leaning in, I pick the folder up first and flip through it, feeling even worse at seeing all the cutouts and receipts and planning that have gone into a wedding that's not going to happen.

"I'll take care of all that," she says.

I glance over my shoulder. "I can help. In fact, let me keep it and I'll take care of it."

She reaches for it and I move it out of her way. "Elena."

"Fine. But you can't take the photo."

This time I make the effort to turn all the way around. "Why would you think I would ever take that from you?"

She shrugs, her tears returning. "Make sure you tell them..." Her breath hitches. "Make sure you tell them how much I love them and how much they mean to me."

Putting the folder under my shitty arm, I extend the other one to grab the frame and hold it up to her. "Their love for you isn't conditional. It isn't only based on you being my fiancée."

She takes the photo out of my hands and stares at it.

"I know it hurts too much now, but whenever you're ready, and no matter how long it takes, go visit them. Because there's no doubt in my mind how happy they'll be to see you."

28

—————

JORDAN

IT HAD BEEN a few days since Gael came over, but I knew he needed some time alone to work through his breakup with Elena. I knew hurting her hurt him just as much, and I wasn't going to be selfish and rush whatever process he was going through in order to forgive himself.

I told him, whenever he was ready, I was here. He needed to take as few or as many steps as he felt up to, because I was here, happy to wait and not planning on going anywhere.

It didn't hurt that I was filled with a new wave of confidence that sustained me now that what happened in Vegas was no longer a painful secret between us.

I knew not remembering bothered him, and I knew my choice not to tell him also hurt, but the truth had tethered me to him in a way that no longer had me worried he was going to slip through my fingers and disappear.

He was mine, and it wasn't just a feeling anymore. I believed it.

My cell vibrates on my desk and a text notification from Gael appears on the screen.

Gael: What are you doing tonight?

I quickly write back.

Me: Whatever it is you're going to ask me to do.

Gael: You're ridiculous. Can I come over?

Me: Since when do you need to ask me to come over?

Gael: It's a yes or no question, Jordan, just answer it.

Me: Yes.

Just to be annoying and hopefully make him smile, I follow up on my last text with another fifteen Yeses, making sure he got the point.

After finally receiving them all, he responds.

Gael: I told you you were ridiculous.

Gael: See you tonight.

My concentration is shot to shit after that small conversation, and when Frankie barges in asking about contracts, I rise up off my chair and decide I've had enough.

"I've got to go," I announce.

"Okayyy," Frankie drawls. "Thank you for letting me know, but also, do you have the contracts?"

"Yes, shit," I answer, a little bit preoccupied. Sliding open my filing cabinet, I pull out the folder he requested and toss it on the desk. "How urgent are those?"

"They can wait, why?"

I walk toward my door and grab my coat and scarf, slipping them on. "Come with me, I need your help with something."

———

IT WAS AMAZING how I could fill journal after journal with all the things Gael and I had done together, but waiting for him to walk through my front door, knowing just how much our lives were going to change from here on out, had to be my most favorite.

I'd sent him a text earlier telling him the front door was open and to come right on in when he got here. I'd never done anything like this for anyone before, and I had no idea what his reaction would be, but I hoped he'd like it.

"Why don't you have any—"

His eyes roam around my open plan living area, taking in my surprise.

February was upon us and the nights were still cold and the sun set early, and the illumination of all the lit candles that decorated my house were the perfect contrast to the dark night around us.

"What's this?" he asks, walking farther into the house, dropping his coat on the couch. "What's going on?"

Slowly, I navigate my steps around the candles and meet him in the middle of the room. I falter with my hands, not knowing if I can touch him and kiss him, or if he still needs space.

But the guesswork is taken away from me when he cradles one side of my face and brings his lips to mine.

My heart sighs in contentment as my mouth tingles for more.

"It feels different and new, but somehow not very different and new at all," he says.

"What's that?"

"Kissing you."

I brush my knuckles down his cheek. "Are you okay?"

"I'm definitely better than I've been in a really long

time." He kisses me again. "Now, tell me what this is all about."

Entwining my fingers with his, I lead him, candles directing us all the way, to my bedroom.

When we pass the threshold and a crestfallen look washes over Gael's face, I know the question before he even has to ask it.

"We didn't," I tell him.

"How did you know?"

"Apart from myself, and even then I get it wrong," I joke, "I don't know anybody else as well as I know you."

"So we didn't..."

"Have sex?" I laugh and shake my head. "No, that first is still yet to come. But regardless, that's not what I brought you in here for."

"It's not?"

"I don't know about you, but I don't need to get knocked in the dick with that hand." I tip my head down at his broken arm.

He sighs. "You have no idea how fucking annoying it is. And now it's getting itchy and it makes me feel like I'm not clean no matter how often I shower."

"Good thing that's what I brought you in here for," I segue.

"Are you saying I smell?"

The look of mortification on his face would be funnier if I weren't out here lining up the inside of my house in candles and trying to figuratively serenade him with a song I'd never sung before. "Can you please stop talking so I can get to the point of this evening? Please?"

He raises our linked hands to his mouth and kisses my knuckles. "I like you like this."

"Like what?"

"Flustered."

Rolling my eyes, I pull him toward my en suite bathroom and push open the door. The bath eagerly awaits its occupant, hot water on standby, the edge lined with enough products to start my own store.

Two plush white robes, that Gael can't wear, hang off the towel hooks attached to my wall. A stack of towels is ready on the nearby shelf, and brand new pajamas sit on the edge of the basin, ready to be worn.

I rest my hands on his hips and prop my chin on his shoulder so he can hear me when I talk.

"Apart from the actual crash and how scary it was to think I could lose you, do you know what I hated the most about your accident?" I take his silence as my cue to continue. "I hated that I couldn't take care of you, in or out of the hospital. All I wanted to do was fuss over you, and I couldn't."

"I wanted to be the one to buy you these oversized flannels you insist on wearing because of your cast, when a t-shirt is probably easier."

"It's cold," he protests. "And I kind of like them."

I press my lips to his neck, his pulse thrumming beautifully underneath his skin. "So, that's what I want to do tonight. Just take care of you. Show you how fucking thankful I am that you're here and with me."

I turn him around, my eyes refusing to look anywhere else but right at him. Shaky fingers find the buttons of his shirt, but I purposefully hold off on unbuttoning them.

"For so long"—my voice is hoarse and thick, the words on my tongue waiting a lifetime to come out—"I have learned to love you from afar, and I'm begging you please, please let me love you up close."

His working hand covers mine, guiding me to help him

take his shirt off, one button at a time. My fingers can't help but skim his skin, relishing in my new reality.

The shirt takes a few tries to get over his cast, but when his whole chest is on display, the struggle was most definitely worth it.

Wordlessly, Gael's eyes dart down to his pants, and I obey his silent command. First is his belt, then I unsnap the button and drag the teeth of the zipper down. The anticipation of seeing him naked again is palpable.

My cock thickens with every sliver of skin my eyes can see. I push his pants down his legs, and he eagerly steps out of them, his underwear still on, his dick visibly hard.

Quickly kissing his cheek, I step around him and turn the faucet to hot and let it run. When the right temperature starts flowing, I plug the drain and fill the tub, adding soapy products along the way.

When I'm satisfied with the way it looks, I turn to find Gael watching me with a dreamlike quality on his face. Hooking my fingers into the waistband of his briefs, I tug him to me so his cock is pressed against mine.

"You ready to get in?" I ask.

"Aren't you a little overdressed?"

I actually had no plans to join him, wanting to restrain myself and allow him actual time to relax, but now, with his body so close, my previous logic seems stupid.

"Are you going to return the favor?" I sass back.

He wastes no time, his hands all over me, pulling my shirt up over my head and pushing my pants down my legs, working diligently despite the awkwardness of the cast. "You were just as eager in Vegas," I say.

"Of course I was," he says gruffly. "I don't need to remember to know you're not the only one who felt like they were loving a man from behind a wall of glass."

The last barrier between us comes off and then I'm climbing into the warm bath waiting for Gael to settle himself between my legs.

"Don't forget to keep your hand out of the water," I remind him. "I bought this chopping board thing that you can rest it on."

Slowly, Gael follows my instructions and sits down, his arm situated perfectly on the edge of the bath. I groan when his skin brushes mine, loving how the bubbles hide the places my hands plan to roam.

"Relax, baby," I whisper.

His head falls back on my shoulder and I casually drop kisses on the column of his neck.

"Don't stop touching me," he says. "Please don't stop."

With no plans to, I do as he asks, using soaps and gels, fascinated by the slick slide over his skin.

I knead his shoulders and wash his back and, when my arms thread through his, he grips my hand and slips it in between his legs. "Make me come," he rasps. "Fuck, I haven't come in so long."

I read between the lines, hearing the exact words he's not saying.

It's been nobody but you.

I wrap my fingers around his shaft. My own erection throbs and presses into his back as I glide my hand up and down his. My fingers roll his nipple as I suck at the skin on his neck, purposefully marking him where the whole world can see.

"Fuuuuck," he rasps. Instinctively, his hips buck, and his ass pushes back against me, rubbing my desperate cock at just the right angle. The water sloshes around us as we both focus on bringing the other pleasure.

"Damn, I'm close," he pants. "Faster."

He angles his head just enough for me to capture his mouth and plunge my tongue inside. We're nothing but heat and desperation as we both rock faster, and I feel his hard body spasm against me.

His orgasm triggers my own, and I groan loudly into his ear as we become surrounded by a mix of water and come and soap.

My body sags against the tub and Gael relaxes against me.

"Damn." He chuckles. "I hope you meant it when you said you wanted to take care of me, because I'm not settling for anything less than that."

I heave a sigh with nothing but a smile on my face. "Let me rinse you off in the shower and show you just how good I can take care of you."

29

———

GAEL

TWO WEEKS LATER

TODAY WAS D DAY, and I meant that both figuratively and literally. I had an appointment with my neurologist in an hour and I was getting this cock block of a cast off my arm straight after.

I was hoping the doctor was going to tell me I was cleared to go back to work and drive, seeing as my headaches were now non-existent. I was advised to get some brain scans done and ensure there wasn't any residual swelling or that a hematoma had formed.

I was nervous, but I felt the best I had in a long time. On all levels.

I knew a lot of that came down to Jordan, but it wasn't just about him as a person and how much I loved him. It was the way being together had impacted us as a couple and individually.

I felt happier and lighter than I had in such a long time. And it saddened me to say it predated the accident, and maybe if I had taken better notice, I would've saved both Elena and myself some heartache.

Considering it had only been official for two weeks now, it should've felt weird to call us a couple. But it felt right.

Together, we were the same but different.

We were and always would be best friends, but the physical and romantic aspects of our relationship took it to levels I had no idea existed.

I still didn't remember Vegas, and I was coming to terms with the fact that the memories of that time we'd spent together were probably never going to come back. Some days that thought bothered me, and others I couldn't care less.

Truth be told, I didn't need the memories. The same way my heart knew it was broken before I did, every part of my body knew Jordan's.

And finally, after a hellish two months, I was going to have both my hands back and be able to touch him properly for nothing less than a full twenty-four hours.

The only thing about today that I wasn't looking forward to was telling my parents that Elena and I had broken up and canceled the wedding. I had told them we were on a break—to explain the recent absence—and they'd been hoping and praying for her return ever since.

My parents knew I had an appointment today and I promised them that I'd come see them after, no matter the results.

Jordan and I hadn't intended to keep our relationship a secret, but after everything we'd been through in such a short span of time, we felt like we needed to take a moment and let it all sink in.

Even though I hated lying to my family, I wasn't going to tell them I cheated on Elena with Jordan. Some people would say I was a coward, but I felt it was something that should remain between the three of us. And if Elena wanted to tell someone, it would be her prerogative.

"Don't forget your X-rays," Jordan says, handing me a steaming mug of coffee and kissing me on the cheek.

Like a lovestruck teenager, I touch my cheek after he's kissed it, still not used to the amount of attention and affection he gives me. It's always something. A reminder here, a note there. Fresh coffee and my favorite food.

He'd even bought me more flannel shirts that I promised to wear just to annoy him even after my cast was off. I was used to being the caretaker, and I enjoyed it, but the way Jordan took care of *me*? That made me want to fuck him and marry him all in the same breath.

I put my coffee down and pointed to the door. "They're over there ready to go with us as well as some stuff I need to drop off at home after we go to Mom and Dad's."

"If you'd just move in, you wouldn't have to keep using your place like a halfway house."

"I'm not halfway to anywhere, thank you. I just think it would be a good idea to tell everyone first."

He finishes off his coffee, rinses the mug, and sets it in the sink. "So you'll move in?"

Walking around the counter, I'm in front of him in a few steps. Fisting the front of his shirt, I drag him to me, a wicked smirk spreading across his lips. "I never said I wouldn't move in. I said not yet. There's a difference."

Grabbing the back of my neck, he pushes me to him, slamming my mouth to his.

"I love you," he murmurs against my mouth, going back and forth for quick kisses. "Are you nervous about today?"

I shrug. "A man could get used to his man waiting on him hand and foot."

A blinding smile stretches across his face. "His man, hey?"

"Would you like to call yourself something else?"

He clicks his tongue and smirks, but I don't need to hear the words to know exactly what he's thinking.

A hand sneaks around my back, squeezing one of my ass cheeks. "Are you ready to go?"

"Yeah," I say more seriously. "Even if they say no to work or driving, at least I get to get this motherfucker off."

"You'll at least get to jerk yourself off now."

"Now why would I do that when you do such a wonderful job."

We continue to laugh and joke, Jordan purposefully trying to take my mind off the appointment.

By the time we park and get inside the medical offices it only takes another five minutes for the secretary to call my name. I hold my hand out to Jordan to join me and he looks surprised. "Are you not coming?"

"Of course." He hops up off the chair and takes my hand. "I didn't come in with you last time, so I didn't know if you still wanted company."

"Last time isn't this time," I tell him, threading my fingers through his. "I always want you by my side."

———

"HOW DO you want to do this?" Jordan asks, reluctantly letting go of my hand.

"First, we could go in the house like we usually do and not hover like we're guests."

"And then?"

My father chooses this moment to open the door,

halting our conversation. "Gael, Jordan. How are you, *mis muchachos?*"

"Hey, Pa," I greet while raising my eyebrows at Jordan. "How are you?"

"I'm good now you two are here." He puts an arm over each of our shoulders. "Now, come and sit and tell us what happened at the doctor's. Your sisters are here too, waiting in the kitchen."

"Of course they are," I groan.

"Think of it this way. We won't have to repeat the story five different times," Jordan says. "Mariana and Laura will tell Seth and Ray."

"Tell Seth and Ray what?" Ray interrupts, appearing from the kitchen.

"Wow." I turn to Jordan. "Does nobody in this family work?"

"Says you two, here on a Friday, off work."

"I actually had a neurologist appointment," I say somberly, knowing he's going to feel bad in five. Four. Three. Two. Annnd...

"Shit, Laura told me about it and I forgot. Is everything okay?"

"Yeah." I tip my head toward the kitchen. "I'll tell everyone when we sit down for lunch."

The eight of us sit around the table, my mom and Mariana finishing up the place settings and laying out all the fillings for the Carne Asada. There's a huge bowl of chips for Jordan in front of his chair because he doesn't eat flour tortillas.

"So, what happened at the doctor's, *mijo?*" My mom takes her seat and leans forward with interest.

"Well." I give Jordan a quick glance, and he's got his

head down, but it's impossible to miss his smile. "He cleared me for work."

The table erupts into cheers.

"And I can drive."

"That's so good, Gael." My mom scoots the chair backward and walks around the table. She throws her arms around my head and squashes me to her. "I'm so happy."

When she releases me, I stick my skinny, pale, no-longer-in-a-cast arm up in the air. "And I got this off."

I felt like a kid showing off all my achievements, but it had been such a relief to hear the doctor say I was in the clear. I was so ready to get back to life and live it, wholly.

Giddiness and nervousness went to battle in my stomach as I tried to work out the best segue to tell everyone about Jordan and me.

"Also, I have one more thing I need to talk to you all about." Something about the tone of my voice forces the cheering to quiet. We all wait for Mom to take her seat and when she does, all eyes are on me.

"Elena and I aren't getting married," I announce evenly.

"What happened?" Mariana asks.

"Lots of things," I answer vaguely. "We just..."

"They weren't the right fit, Mariana," my mom says, surprising me, the tone of her voice letting on she probably knew a whole lot more about my relationship than I thought she did. "They tried to make it work, but they weren't the right fit."

My mom then shifts her gaze from Mariana to me. "Is she okay?"

I nod, even though I don't really know if she is. I have all the faith in the world that in time she will be.

"And you?"

Finally able to use my right hand, I reach for Jordan, in

broad daylight, without a single care in the world. "I'm really good."

It didn't take them being rocket scientists for each of them to put two and two together and figure out, with how close Jordan and I had always been, there may have been an overlap. But thankfully, none of them ask the questions.

I wanted to scream from the rooftops that I was in love with Jordan and that my love for him wasn't new and it had never waned, but I didn't need to worry about that today.

A time would come where the story unfolded and everyone would know just how long we'd loved each other and how deep it ran.

He winks at me, mouthing "I love you," and I couldn't control myself even if I'd wanted to try. Leaning over, I kiss him softly. Gently. Enough that it says "I love you" back, but not too much that it scares my family.

Reluctantly, I move away and we both look around, taking in the six pairs of eyes that are staring at us. If I expected anger and disappointment, there was none to be found. It was nothing but love and happiness and support. Support I didn't think I deserved. Support I was so blessed to have. Like they were proud of me.

Why I thought they would react differently, I'll never know.

"Um..." Seth interrupts the moment and raises his hand. "This might be really bad timing, but I have questions."

"You have questions?" my sister repeats, not at all impressed.

"Does this mean you're bisexual? Or are you gay?"

It's always my brothers-in-law making shit weird.

"I can't say I've thought about it, to be honest."

"But if you did think about it, which way would you lean?"

I look over at Mariana. "Seriously with this guy?"

She shrugs. "We've been married too long, I don't have the time to find someone else I'm comfortable enough farting in front of."

Jordan laughs from beside me while Seth taps the table. "We're getting off topic. Gael, can you please answer?"

"If I must, I would go with bisexual."

"Booyah," Ray screams, shooting out of his seat. "That's twenty Benjamins for me, baby."

"What the hell are you talking about?" Laura asks her husband.

"Seth and I have been waiting for these two to hurry up with this shit," he explains. "We put ten dollars away every time we caught one of you obsessively staring at the other."

"And it only happened two hundred times?" Jordan asks. "Why didn't you guys say something?"

"Definitely happened more than that," Seth answers. "But we were going to go broke. And if we'd said something, you wouldn't have listened anyway."

"But I don't understand. How do you decide who gets the money if you both thought the same thing was going to happen?"

"We bet whether you would come out as gay or bisexual when it happened."

"That's fucking ridiculous," I mutter.

Ray comes around the table, standing behind Jordan and me. He puts a hand on either side of our heads and pushes them together, roughly bringing them to his chest. He plants a loud dramatic kiss on the top of each of our heads. "Nothing's ridiculous, lover boys, everything's fucking perfect."

30

JORDAN

THE DRIVE between my house and Emilio and Maria's was only twenty minutes long, but when I had Gael's hand running up and down my thigh and his fingers purposefully grazing my erection, the time it took between both places felt never-ending.

I capture his hand with mine as I focus all my other attention on the road. "Are you trying to kill me?" I ask.

"If killing you means getting you worked up just enough that you throw yourself at me when we get home, then yes, that's exactly what I'm doing."

My mind snags on the word home. "When we get home, hey?"

I glance between him and the road, loving the soft smile that spreads across his lips.

"I know you don't like my place," he starts.

I try to protest and clarify exactly what it is and isn't that I like, but the bottom line is, he's right. It's not my favorite place. I can't help but associate it with a time when I resented him and our circumstances, and forgive me if I don't want to be reminded of that every time I eat and sleep there.

"And I respect that and understand why," he continues, his hand never losing stride. "So I have a proposition for you."

I raise an eyebrow at him. "I'm listening."

"I'll move in with you on the condition that we start looking for a place to move into that's ours."

I let the word "ours" ruminate in my mind and roll it around on my tongue. "I can get behind that idea."

He squeezes my thigh. "You won't mind leaving your place? I know how much you love it and how much work you put into it."

In perfect timing, I pull into my driveaway, switch the car off, and turn to face Gael.

"I do love this place," I say. "I love it because it represents the man I was when I bought it and the place that allowed me to grow into the man I am now."

"And what kind of man is that?"

Whether he notices or not, Gael's body leans a little closer, hovering over the center console, my answer to his question distracting enough to stop his hand from moving.

For some reason my mind takes me back to the first time I saw him in the hospital, all the scratches and bruises on his beautiful face.

My fingers itch to touch him, and I find myself tracing all the places that have now healed, staring into brown eyes that felt like they were closed for so long. "A man whose love is reciprocated. A man whose days are bright and future is full. A man who could be a husband and maybe a father."

Gael interrupts me, kissing me softly on the lips. "Definitely a father."

"Definitely a father then," I whisper, kissing him back. "I'm the kind of man who has loved his best friend for a lifetime and hopes he gets to love him for a million more."

I hear the click of his seat belt unclipping and then feel the release of my own.

"House," he grinds out. "Now."

We both dart out of the car. I fumble with my keys as Gael's hot breath hits the back of my neck, and goosebumps cover my skin.

It's always like this with him. As soon as the thought hits, he goes from zero to a hundred, absolutely raring to go. And I can't say I hate it, because when his hands and mouth are on me, desperate and needy, he makes me feel like I'm the air he needs to breathe.

The keys eventually cooperate and we tumble past the threshold, my lips on his, his hands in my hair.

With his cast off, the first thing on his list was sex. Uninterrupted—not awkward maneuvering, both hands available for use—sex. It would be our first time together, and the thought alone made me feel anxious and inexperienced.

It's not like we hadn't ravaged each other in every other way possible, but this was new for him in ways it wasn't for me and, even if my subconscious told me it was the least of *his* worries, it didn't mean I hadn't added it to the short list of mine.

Refusing to part, our lips stay fused as we shed a piece of clothing with every step we take. Winter made it feel like you were unwrapping a present with every added layer.

We kick off our shoes and drag out belts. At one point, I hear something rip and I don't know if it was his shirt or mine. I also don't care.

By the time we reach our room, we're both naked, hard, and breathless.

"I want to fuck you," he says between kisses. "And then I want you to fuck me."

"We have time for all of that."

"But I don't know which one I want first."

Not surprised, I chuckle as I push him farther into the room. "Always so damn impatient." I give his ass a little slap. "Get on the bed."

His hand reaches for his thick cock, stroking it, the second his back hits the middle of the bed.

I quickly detour to the bathroom and come back with the lube, tossing it on the mattress beside him.

Climbing up on the bed, I hover over him on all fours. Gael fists my cock, and his eyes twinkle in amusement, clearly thinking *I couldn't do this with my cast on.*

I drop my mouth to his, teasing him with a slow, languid kiss, a complete opposite to the speed of his hands as he jerks us off.

Placing his palm on my chest, he gives me a subtle push. I peer down at him.

"I want to fuck you," he says again, his eyes blazing, his voice final.

Nodding, I follow his lead as he releases his hold on me, grabs the lube, and pushes himself up the bed enough to have his head and neck propped up by our pillows.

Straddling him, I lower myself atop his thighs. He spreads his legs underneath me, arranging me a little wider.

"Kiss me," he demands.

I wrap a hand around both of our cocks as my mouth descends to his chest, kissing, moving up to his shoulder and across his collarbone. My lips dance on his skin, up his neck and along the shape of his jaw.

Big firm hands land on my ass, kneading and squeezing,

and when my mouth lands on his, he ghosts his fingers down my crease.

Our kiss deepens as my strokes get faster and his touch becomes firmer. There's a momentary absence and then Gael's hand returns to my ass and slick, cool fingers slip in between my cheeks. My breath hitches at the temperature change, and I groan when the pad of his finger spreads lube against my hole.

He teases and tortures, alternating between circling my rim and pushing his fingertip in and out of me.

"More," I groan, breaking the kiss. "More."

His finger gets deeper and my strokes fumble, the promise of more tripping me up. When he adds a second digit, my hands drop beside me, keeping me steady. I instinctively push back on him, wanting more.

"Fuck, I love you like this." His voice is thick and husky. "Needy and desperate. I can't wait to feel you around me, watch you completely unravel."

Adding another finger, he grazes my prostate and my body shudders in anticipation.

"Lube me up," he commands.

The best thing about Gael having his cast on and deciding to wait was being able to get tested and have the all clear before tonight.

I drizzle the lube up and down his cock, and when he slips his fingers out of me, I push in my own using the excess.

"So damn impatient," Gael says with a smirk, repeating my words from earlier. "Move your fingers."

The last two weeks have been days upon days of endless exploration. There isn't anything he won't try and I've loved being his teacher, but as I make way for him and his crown nudges my hole, I am fully aware that someone should've prepared me for *this*.

Gael slowly pushes inside me, our eyes locked, as inch by inch he gets deeper and deeper.

The fact we're skin to skin, nothing in between, only intensifies the depth and the pleasure. When he completely bottoms out, I groan and my body arches from the delicious burn of the intrusion.

"Fuck. Jordan. This feels amazing." He begins to move his hips. "*You* feel amazing."

My body rises and falls on his cock, loving the stretch and the fullness; completely consumed by Gael and his body.

With every thrust, words spill from his mouth, blanketing my skin and seeping into my bones.

I need you.

I want you.

I love you.

"Harder, Gael," I pant. "Harder."

He jackknifes his hips into me, and the deep angle hits perfectly. Grabbing my cock, I frantically jerk myself off, squeezing my balls, spreading my pre-come down my length, making my strokes fast and easy.

"You ready to come?" Managing only a nod, but needing *something*, I slam my mouth to his. Tangling my tongue with his, I pour every ounce of love I have for him into the kiss and feel every part of him echo it all right back.

My hand moves faster as Gael's thrusts become crazed and hurried.

"Gael," I call out. "Gael, Gael, Gael."

Like a slingshot, every muscle in my body is pulled back, taut and tight in preparation.

"That's it, baby," he coaxes, keeping his gaze on mine. "I got you. Come with me."

As his cock repeatedly hits my prostate, pushing me further off the edge, it's his words and the adoration in his eyes that lure the release out of me.

"Fuck, Gael," I cry out as thick, sticky ropes of come paint my hands.

When his hips piston one last time, I feel his body tremble beneath me, his come pulse inside me, and hear his groan of pleasure all around me.

It's complete ecstasy.

Exhausted, yet sated, I drop my head onto his shoulder, both of us catching our breath.

All the words feel inadequate as Gael's fingers trail up and down the knobs of my spine. And when his come begins to leak out of me, neither one of us runs to move.

"I love you so much," he says softly. "Sometimes I feel like my chest is about to burst from how much I feel for you."

I angle my head to look at him and I catch his gaze.

"I'll let you love me for a million lifetimes," he says. "As long as I can love you for a million more."

31

GAEL

A HAND CURLS around my waist and another appears in front of my face holding a bottle of beer. "Your mom and dad are here," Jordan says.

I stop mashing up the avocados for the guacamole, accept the drink on offer, and take a sip. "Is there a reason you're in here telling me and they're not in here?"

"I could be wrong, but I think your mom is still upset you told her not to bring any food to our housewarming party."

Huffing, I put the fork down and turn in his arms. "Firstly, it's a dinner. Our family, Deacon and Julian, and Frankie, are not a party. And secondly, can you please tell me how 'Mom, I want you to come and relax, because you're always the one hosting' is the same as 'don't bring any food'?"

He shrugs. "I'm not exactly sure, but I'm going to tell her your guacamole tastes like shit and she needs to save the day and then I've got something I need to show your dad."

"My guacamole doesn't taste like shit," I say flatly.

"That's not the point of the story, baby." He points at

the counter with all the ingredients. "Maybe ruin it so my story is plausible."

Continuing to squash the avocados, I hear Jordan leave and wait for my mom to come and call me out for the lie. Considering she's the one who taught me how to make it, there's a high chance she'll know Jordan's lying.

It only takes a handful of minutes for the kitchen door to swing open, and I know it's my mom because she has the softest, quietest footsteps known to man.

"Hey, Ma," I greet casually, pretending I don't know she's upset with me.

When she doesn't answer, I turn around and find her dabbing her eyes with a tissue. "Ma, what's wrong?"

No longer interested in making my guacamole, I leave the utensils on the counter and walk over to her. "Are you really that upset that I told you not to cook?"

"No." She slaps me lightly on the chest. "I mean, I was upset, but that's not what I'm crying about. These are happy tears."

Relieved, I wrap my arm around her shoulder and kiss her on the top of her head. "Who or what are your happy tears for?"

"For you, *mijo*." She steps out of my hold and gestures around the room. "Look at this beautiful place. You and Jordan are making it a home. I'm just so proud of you. Both of you."

I don't know what it's like for other people, but every time my mom or dad told me they were proud of me, I basked in that love and attention for as long as I could.

Especially after what happened between Elena and me.

Even though Jordan and I are blissfully happy, I carried my regret over cheating on Elena every day.

And I think my mother knows that.

She often reminds me that the cost of happiness is high. Sometimes we hurt people, and often other people hurt us. It wasn't ideal, but it was necessary, because we'd never be able to truly comprehend the weight and importance of our happiness if we didn't work hard to get it.

"Thank you, Ma," I say. "I'm proud of us too."

"You should be. Nothing makes me happier than seeing my four children happy."

Four children.

If I could love her more for the way she loved Jordan, I would.

As if thinking about him conjured him up, Jordan walks through the kitchen door, eyeing us both. "Is it safe in here?"

"I don't know," my mom says. "I still haven't tried the guacamole."

———

"SO, did you just come to my house for dinner so you can sit on your phone?" I nudge Frankie's foot under the table and he tears his eyes away from the cell and then shifts them to me. "I'm sorry, it's all Jordan's fault anyway, he told me to try online dating, but I didn't know this many dick pics were part of the experience."

A hand covers my eyes. "The only dick you're allowed to see is mine."

I pull Jordan's hand away from my eyes and tilt my head to kiss him as he takes a seat beside me. "Don't worry, yours is all I need anyway."

"Yeah," Frankie interrupts, pointing at us. "This is the reason this friendship of ours is never going to work. Every time I look at you two, all I do is remember how fucking single I am."

It was hilarious how Frankie had so seamlessly fit into our lives. Once I got over my jealousy, which took a little bit longer than I'd like to admit, Jordan made the decision to assign him as our realtor and we actually hit it off really well.

He listened to things I said I wanted in a house. Things I didn't want. When we needed an objective opinion, he was the one to help sway the vote.

And despite the rocky start between us, it's so obvious he's been a great friend to Jordan. Especially when he needed him most.

"So you haven't had *any* luck?" Jordan asks him.

Locking his phone, he puts it down in front of him and gives us his complete attention. "Actually, there is this one guy, but it kind of sounds too good to be true, so there's a chance I'll still bail on him."

"Uncle Gael. Uncle Jordan." My niece, Lucia, skips over with Sara in tow, looking very contemplative and serious.

"Do you know how we're going to Disneyland soon, to use our Christmas present?"

"Yeah…" I answer cautiously, almost certain we're walking into a trap.

"We've been talking." I have to bite my bottom lip to stop myself from laughing, because by "we," she means she and Sara have turned Nico and Alejandro into their minions, making them play and talk about whatever they want. "And we think Uncle Jordan should buy us that present every year."

"Lucia," Laura calls out as Jordan says, "I'd love to, *princesa.*"

Ignoring my sister, Lucia smiles and holds out her hand. "It's a deal. Let's shake on it."

They do, and I'm left staring at Jordan, speechless.

"What?" he asks self-consciously.

"Nothing," Frankie retorts, "Besides the fact that girl just played you. She and Sara are high-fiving as we speak."

"It's no big deal, they'll probably forget by next Christmas anyway."

He was right, they might be enamored by some new fad or trend by the time Christmas came around, but my gut told me it would be Jordan who wouldn't forget.

He presses his lips to my cheek. "I actually came here to ask if you wanted to open your present before dessert or wait until after."

Confused, my eyes dart around to everyone who's now watching us. "Why are there presents?"

"It's your birthday next week," he says, as if that alone explains it. "And last time I checked, I actually didn't need a reason to buy you a present."

I roll my eyes at him. "Fine, we can do it now."

Giddy, he jumps up off the chair, and I watch him retreat down the hall and into our guest bedroom. When he returns with three decent sized packages, I'm left wondering how he made this happen right under my nose.

"Okay, you can open whichever you want first," he informs me. "But before you do, I want you to know that Ray and Seth helped me out a lot with these, and Julian and Deacon talked me off the ledge about whether or not it was a terrible idea."

It wasn't often that I got to see Jordan flustered, and this had me eager to see what was underneath the wrapping even more.

He hands me one gift and it's rectangular in shape and somewhat heavy.

I slip my finger underneath the layer of wrapping paper and slide it across where the tape has sealed the ends together, tearing it open with a clean cut.

Carefully removing the paper, I'm shocked to see a photo of Jordan and me, hugging and laughing, blown up and mounted in the frame.

"When was this?" I whisper. But even as the question leaves my mouth, I know there is only one reason I wouldn't remember taking a photo with Jordan, no matter how many years ago it was. "Is this…"

He nods, and I take in the nervous way he chews on the inside of his cheek.

"Can I open the other ones?"

Giving me room, Jordan steps away as I open the other two, both the frames the same in sizing and weight as the first one.

The second one is almost like the person taking the photo kept pressing the button to capture the images, even after we stopped posing. But we look so happy, my head back, laughing, Jordan staring at me the way he always does.

With love and reverence, it was the exact same look I remembered from over the years, but in this photo, there was no hiding it, there was no wistful longing. In this photo, he loved me for the world to see, with no plans of letting me go.

Overcome with emotion, I take a shaky breath, trying not to cry, and reach for the third one and open it slowly, trying to savor the moment.

When the wrapping paper falls to the floor, I can't stop the tears this time.

The third one is similar to the second one, candid and a

little blurry around the edges, but the slight differences are there to see. It's Jordan who is laughing this time, and I have my head tilted to the side, staring at him, with a dopey smile on my face, showing my wonderment.

"These are beautiful," I manage, torn between staring at the Jordan in my photos and the Jordan in front of me. "I love them so much."

"I know Vegas is a hard place for us to mentally return to sometimes. For a number of reasons, good and bad." He swallows hard, and I watch the myriad of emotions that cross his face as he tries to string out a sentence without crying. "Whether you remember it or not, whether or not we wish things happened differently, the crux of the matter is, what we have now started in these pictures."

I run my fingers across the glass, tracing the silhouettes of our bodies. These photos encapsulate my love for this man perfectly. My smile and the way my eyes lit up for him.

I knew that smile. I knew that look. And I was one hundred percent sure, even without my memory, I knew how hard my heart would've been beating for him at that moment.

"A few months ago, Ray pulled me aside telling me about a bunch of photos he took on his phone in Vegas. He had also mentioned it to Seth, who ended up telling me he too had photos. But after everything happened, he'd forgotten they even existed." Jordan looks over at Seth and Ray. "I think I made fun of them no less than twenty times for taking so many weird photos on that trip."

Glancing back at me, he raises a hand to my cheek. "I know you don't always love the elaborate public declarations of love, but I know you know, I don't know how to love you quietly. I don't know how to keep all the feelings I have for you inside."

What he didn't say for everybody else to hear was that after years of keeping it all hidden and to himself, he refused to do it. When he felt it, he wanted to say it then and there, and I would never take that away from him.

"But everyone here is a part of our story. The good times and the hard times," he continues. "And I just wanted to give you something because I could. Because sometimes I know not being able to remember bothers you. And because I can't wait to stare at these photos in our new home every damn day."

At this, everyone laughs, and I'm sitting here wondering how the hell I got so lucky. Looking down at the photo and then back at Jordan, I shake my head at him, but the smile on my face continues to grow. "You're completely ridiculous, you know that?"

He winks. "You tell me often."

I wipe at my eyes and carefully place the frame down on the floor beside me. Scooting closer to him, I grab his face roughly, on purpose, and I smash my mouth to his.

It's not enough. It never is, but it'll have to do until I have him alone and naked and completely at my mercy later tonight.

Because while he loves loudly with his words, I love hard with my body.

That's how it usually works for us. But sometimes things need to be said. Need to be heard, only for me to reiterate them at night and make sure he feels them in my touch too.

This was one of those times.

Not wanting to lose my nerve with our audience, I lean my head back just enough that his face is the only thing I see. "Sometimes I think I don't tell you enough how much I love you. Or I take for granted that you just know. I've also known you long enough to know you're grateful to anyone who loves you. And that's not how it's supposed to be.

"Because loving you, in any capacity, is easy. But falling and staying in love with you is inevitable. There were bumps and bruises and breaks on the way, but there wasn't any other choice."

My gaze darts between his eyes. "There *isn't* any other choice, for either of us. We know that now."

"I love you," I breathe out. "I have loved you on the days you told me I couldn't. I have loved you on the days that I shouldn't. And I will love you for all the days to come."

EPILOGUE
GAEL

ONE YEAR LATER

"OKAY, but when Lucia said 'Can we go to Disneyland every year, Uncle Jordan.' You were not supposed to agree," I whine.

The heat is absolutely suffocating as we wait with the crowd to see some sort of Avengers parade. Sara, Nico, Lucia and Alejandro all hold one of our hands, waiting patiently, while their parents are back at the hotel enjoying a child free day, on us.

"When have you ever known me to withhold anything from those kids?" he looks around and then lowers his mouth to my ear. "And I didn't see you complaining last night when you fucked me on the hotel california king bed after the complimentary couples massage."

"That's beside the point," I retort. "This." I wave my hand around the busy theme park. "It's too much."

"It's never too much," he says. "Plus I was hoping we could start a tradition of sorts that we could continue when our kids come along."

"Wait what?" I stop mid stride. "When *our* kids come along? What are you talking about?"

"I think it's time," he says casually.

I can't help but laugh, "It's time," I repeat. "Just like that, huh?"

And that's how we were. We made general plans. Plans that consisted of a mere mention of what we wanted and the direction we wanted to take, without ever worrying ourselves with the exactness of it all.

It's why we never talk about marriage or kids or houses, until we do.

"To clarify," I start "How would these family traditions go?"

"We would bring the kids." He raises the hands he's holding so I know he's referring to the ones with us now and not our future children. "Every year. No matter what was on, we would always make time for this family holiday."

And then we would have kids and bring them along, and these four will be big enough to show them around. Sharing what they've done, what rides they've been on. You know?"

I did know. I also knew this was the vaguest explanation for something he had clearly been thinking of for a very long time.

But I let him have it, because I could see it. The years passing, the kids growing. The fighting and screaming that came with kids growing and then protectiveness and loyalty that followed.

In the last year, Jordan and I had been living our very best life. We had been in one another's life for almost two decades and this was the happiest either one of us had ever been.

It was a high like no other, Every day undoubtedly better than the one before.

"I'm going to ask a question I already know the answer to, but humor me. Have you thought about how we will be having said children?"

"I thought I would bring it up to you first," he says. But he also isn't looking at me. I tug on his arm and he turns to me with a shit eating grin on his face.

"Why don't I pretend I believe you, and you brought it up to me, and now I'm asking what do our options look like?"

His expression is serious for a second. "Are you sure?"

I look at the kids on either side of us and back at him. "I don't know if this is the worst place to have this conversation, or the best, but of course, I'm sure."

I maneuver the kids so they're standing in front of us, and I move myself closer to him, making sure there's no way he can't hear what I'm about to tell him. "I have always known you've wanted kids, and a big family, and I want them too... and not just because do." I inch closer trying to contend with the noise. "I want to see you be the father you deserved."

I notice the clench in his jaw and the way his throat works over as he processes my words. A small wet laugh leaves his mouth. "I really should've picked a better time to have this conversation."

I shrug to lighten the mood. "Talking about kids in Disneyland seems appropriate."

He glances down at the kids, making sure they're okay and he releases Sara's hand just to give me a quick tight reassuring squeeze.

"I love you," I tell him. "Now tell me our options."

Because of the bustle around us, he's very brief, but the excitement when he's talking has me not wanting to wait another day before taking the leap.

"I'm completely fine with adoption or surrogacy," he advises. "There's no preference for me."

"Well that's settled then. We'll start working out what suits us best when we get back home."

"That's it," he says. "Nothing else to add."

"About children? No. But make sure you're prepared for all the 'why aren't you married' questions when we get back home."

"Actually, why aren't we married?"

"No, Jordan," I say firmly. "We are not having this conversation in Disneyland."

"No we're not getting married and you don't want to tell me why in Disneyland? Or no we're not talking about getting married in Disneyland."

Closing my eyes, I pinch the bridge of my nose. "The latter."

"Oh Ok." I feel his lips on my cheek. "That's fine. We'll talk about it later then."

"Yes. We'll talk about it later."

And that's how it was with us. Easy. Effortless. Endless. Friends. Family. A future.

THE END

———

Did you enjoy Ache?

For more Jordan and Gael, visit my website for their bonus epilogue.

http://www.marleyvbooks.com/bonus-epilogues/

without you
marley valentine

Tragedy brought us together, but something stronger made me want to stay.

Julian was the boy next door. My brother's best friend, he fit with my family in ways I never could. While he and Rhett went on to play house, I left the only life I knew, desperate for a fresh start.

Until everything changed.

Heartache came along, and the aftermath of my brother's death was here to stay. I was now face to face with Julian more than I ever wanted to be.

Being around him brought up all my insecurities, forced me to deal with hard truths, and conjured up feelings I had no business entertaining. He wasn't the man I thought I knew. He was complex and layered, and inherently beautiful in all the ways I'd never noticed.

Not on another person.

Not on another man.

Not until him.

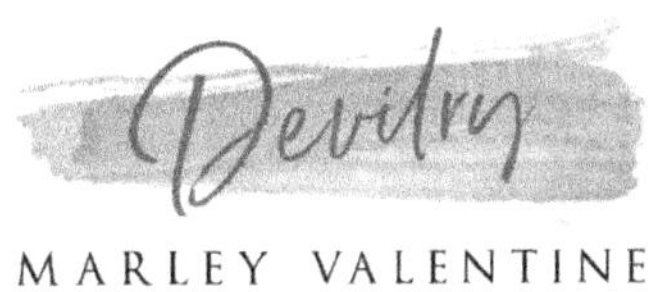

MARLEY VALENTINE

Attending King University was at the top of my bucket list. Falling in love with my professor wasn't.

Earning a full scholarship to King University was my hard earned ticket out of hell. I'm happy to be away from the small town I grew up in and all the equally small minded people who live there.

King was going to be my safe haven. A place where I could leave the old me behind and finally grow into the young man my family had desperately tried to hide away.

Diving head first into new experiences, new friends, and parties, I didn't expect to run straight into the one thing I wasn't ready for.

His arms are welcoming, his body is addictive and his lips are heaven. Cole Huxley is everything I could fall in love with, except for one problem… I never wanted to fall for my professor.

ACKNOWLEDGMENTS

To my wonderful, supportive family, I love you. Thank you for stepping in when I'm too immersed in my books and always helping me get over the finish line. Andrew, you'e the reason I believe in romance. Steph you are the best sister I could ever ask for. And couldn't do any of it without either of you.

Jaxon, my beautiful boy, love you. Always.

Chip and Alexx, it's hard work looking for book covers, but this photo totally found ME. Thank you for the photo, but more importantly thank you for the friendship.

Sybil. My Sipho! I absolutely love you and I love this cover. I can't wait for the next one, so you can love me, hate me and then love me again.

To Marley's Mofo's. You are the BEST reader group a girl could ask for. Thank you for all your encouragement and support. For always showing up and sharing your love for my books. It means the world to me, and I hope you all love this book as much as the ones before.

My street team. You ladies kick ass, each and every day. Thank you for your faith and support.

Book Nerd Services, Greys Promotions and Gay Romance Reviews. Thank you for all your work with ARC's, cover reveal, and release day promotions.

Serious talk, this book almost broke me and not because of the actual story, but because I wanted to give up, right when I couldn't. I didn't really know how I was going to make it to the end, but as always there are a handful of women who have my back and support me—no matter what.

This book wouldn't be what it is without any of you. Jodi, Laura, Kacey, Layla, Shauna and Beth. Thank you for the late nights, the pep talks, the kick up the bum when I needed it, and of course your invaluable friendship.

And thank YOU, for picking this book up, reading my stories, loving them, or even hating them.

Until next time.
Much Peace and Love.

ABOUT THE AUTHOR

Living in Sydney, Australia with her family, Marley Valentine is a USA Today bestselling author and a former social worker who uses her past experiences to write real life, emotional and heartfelt contemporary romance.

She enjoys mixing it up with both M/F and M/M Romance incorporating all forms of life, lust and love as her characters embark on their journey to their happily ever after.

When she's not busy writing her own stories, she spends most of her time immersed in the words of her favourite authors.

Marley enjoys interacting with her readers so please feel free to reach out to her via Facebook, Instagram, email and/or subscribe to her newsletter.

Other Books by Marley Valentine

Light My Way | Find My Way | Reclaim | Revive | Rectify

Love & War

MM Romance Books

Devilry | Without You | Unforgettable (Vino & Veritas)

Find Marley

Facebook | Facebook Reader Group | Amazon Author Page | Goodreads Author Page | Twitter | Instagram | Website | BookBub | Newsletter

www.ingramcontent.com/pod-product-compliance
Lightning Source LLC
Chambersburg PA
CBHW070547120726
47909CB00007B/2271